13
Lovely Frights
for
Lonely Nights

by
Blythe Ayne

13 Lovely Frights for Lonely Nights

Blythe Ayne

Emerson & Tilman, Publishers
129 Pendleton Way #55
Washougal, WA 98671

13 Lovely Frights for Lonely Nights

ebook ISBN: 978-1-947151-62-8
Paperback ISBN: 978-1-947151-63-5
Hardbound ISBN: 978-1-947151-64-2

[1. FICTION / Magical Realism
2. FICTION / Fantasy / Dark Fantasy
3. FICTION / Short Stories (single author)]

BIC: FM
First Edition

13
Lovely Frights
for
Lonely Nights

by
Blythe Ayne

Books & Audio by Blythe Ayne

Fiction:
EOS

The Darling Undesirables Series:
The Heart of Leo - short story prequel
The Darling Undesirables
Moons Rising
The Inventor's Clone
Heart's Quest

Novellas & Short Story Collections:
5 Minute Stories
13 Lovely Frights for Lonely Nights
When Fields Hum And Glow

Children's Illustrated Books:
The Rat Who Didn't Like Rats
The Rat Who Didn't Like Christmas

Nonfiction:
Love Is The Answer
45 Ways To Excellent Life
Horn of Plenty–The Cornucopia of Your Life
Finding Your Path, Engaging Your Purpose

How to Save Your Life Series:
Save Your Life With The Power Of pH Balance
Save Your Life With The Phenomenal Lemon
Save Your Life with Stupendous Spices
Save Your Life with the Elixir of Water

Absolute Beginner Series:
Bed Yoga – Easy, Healing, Yoga Moves You Can Do in Bed
Write Your Book! Publish Your Book! Market Your Book!

Photography & Poetry:
Life Flows on the River of Love
Home & the Surrounding Territory

Audio:
The Power of pH Balance –
Dr. Blythe Ayne Interviews Steven Acuff

Blythe Ayne's physical books & ebooks are found wherever books are sold.
www.BlytheAyne.com

Table of Contents

Stories in ***13 Lovely Frights for Lonely Nights***
have been previously published in the following venues:

From time travel, to a terrifying desert Jinn, to a fractal journey to the next life, these adventures will take you to places you've never been.

Enjoy the ride….

Djinneyah & Co.

I was still in my office in the social science complex at eleven o'clock one night working on a paper that hated me, when I succumbed to the call of a dark chocolate Milky Way. I headed downstairs to the vending machines. There stood E.J., drinking a soda.

I hadn't expected to see any other living thing. I thought about how awful I must look and considered making my escape, but in the moment I hesitated he turned and looked at me. I ran my fingers through my standing-on-end hair, and fed the candy machine a bunch of change.

"Are you in archeology?" He had an accent I couldn't place, faintly Mediterranean I thought, but his pale coloring didn't match.

I shook my head, intent while the machine dropped my chocolate fix. "Anthropology." I grabbed the Milky Way. Even with my mouth watering, I demurred from ripping it open in front of the blond, blue-eyed stranger.

The ugly fluorescent lighting made E.J.'s face flat and sallow, and the dark circles under his eyes looked like bruises, taking the life out of his eyes.

I hoped I looked at least as well and half as good.

"I have to get a paper done by Friday, but I'm stuck in writer's block," he said.

"Yeah. Same here. Exactly. Paper. Friday. Not good." I fingered my candy bar.

He extended his hand. "I'm Elias, but everyone calls me E.J."

I took his hand. Firm, thin, nice. "Ashley. Everyone calls me—Ashley."

E.J. smiled. "You're cute."

"Really?" I thought, cute? *ick* ....

"I mean," E.J. went on, "If you're like me, you're very tired, but still, you're friendly. I've seen you in the halls and you seemed so serious. By the way, you're not only cute, you're beautiful."

"Thank you!" Yes, I liked this appraisal much better. I thought of myself as serious, and who didn't like to be called beautiful once in a while? Particularly when feeling like a rag, a bone, and a hank of hair. "Well, I suppose I'd better get back to work. I only have one more night I can abuse myself with that wretched paper." I moved toward the stairs.

"What's your office phone number?" he asked.

"1233." Hey, why be coy?

He called on Monday, after I, for one, had slept away the better part of the week-end.

We were married five months later.

I didn't realize until after we were married that what had infatuated me about him was not "him" because in that five months of eighteen-hour days working at our graduate degrees I never really found out who "he" was.

I was intrigued by his ethnographic stories—which for him were simply talking about his family, his life. I was fascinated by his ethnographic mix, a blue-eyed blond with an Israeli passport, Arabian blood, and Christian religion. Mostly, I was infatuated with his infatuation with me.

But after we were married, it didn't take me long to learn that love was not infatuation, fascination, or intrigue.

I found out that E.J., as a person, insisted on sleeping on the same side of the bed as I was my habit, that the fact that he never ate what I ate in restaurants was more of a problem when he didn't want to eat what I cooked. I found out that although E.J. was Christian, he took his religion far more seriously and to much greater lengths of ritual and commitment than my live-and-let-live doctrine. Conversely, I couldn't stir him to political fervor—he said American politics were magnificent in concept and pathetic in practice. I discovered I didn't like his friends, and he couldn't stand mine.

I'd never been taught what married love was, not in the way I visualize people in tribal lives sitting down with their young people and imparting the wisdom and art of living with someone and loving them, whether the two of you agree or disagree. The only socialization I'd been given about marriage was to watch my parents fight, become silent, divorce.

No wonder I was going through an internal litany of ambivalence as I packed in preparation for the semester dig E.J. and I were about to embark on in his homeland. It was because he'd been chosen to go on the dig that we decided to get married right away. We didn't want to be apart for four months, and people on the dig were allowed to take spouses. This was a fabulous career and education opportunity, I told myself. I'd be able to do anthropology and archeology. Who'd pass that up?

When we first arrived in Israel we spent a few days with E.J.'s mother and two unmarried adult sisters. The sisters pinched me and stared at me when I laughed. E.J. told me they thought I was too skinny to bear children, and they wanted to be sure I had most of my own teeth. They fed me to the gills six times a day. I was relieved when we left.

E.J. said I met with family approval, even if I was "one of those American women." I restrained myself from saying approval went two ways. I dreaded the thought of future pinching sessions with in-laws. I didn't say anything critical about his family, but I could see E.J. was hurt by my lack of enthusiasm. Problem number one.

Problem number two cropped up that night after we'd arrived at the dig site. We were provided with our own two-room tent which I found charming and romantic. And there were actual American fiberglass Port-a-potties off at a short distance. I'd done my share of camping, so this was a great adventure. But much to my surprise, E.J. started complaining as soon as he saw the bevy of tents in one place and the Port-a-potties in another.

"I can't believe they expect a person to go hiking, just to relieve themselves."

"A little fresh air won't hurt you." I said, unpacking, preoccupied with making the best use of limited space.

"Why couldn't they put one of those facilities by each tent?"

"That'd smell great in a day or two." I started to put things away. I stopped unpacking. "You've been on digs before."

"Two summers in Colorado. We stayed in a motel."

"Jeez," I said, awed by his inexperience. "Better get used to it, Mr. Archaeologist. Anyway, this is a dream come true, a dig in your own country. Real Indiana Jones stuff."

"*Humph.*"

About three a.m. E.J. woke me up with a whispered urgency.

"Wh-what's wrong?" I felt disoriented and frightened by his tone of voice.

"Nothing. I just wondered if you have to go to the bathroom."

"Given how soundly I was sleeping, I don't think so, no."

"Are you sure? I though if you needed to, I'd walk with you."

"No. Don't need to." I closed my eyes. E.J. didn't leave. I kept my eyes closed.

"I—I want some company."

"Come on, E.J., let me sleep." Then I replayed the tone of his voice, which had something in it I'd never heard before. Flat out fear.

I lugged myself out of the comfort of the sway-bottomed cot and stuck my feet into my thongs. "Let's go."

We didn't say anything as we ambled to the port-a-potties. The night was clean-edged as a new knife. The sky seemed different—the stars looked larger, whiter, sharper, and the velveteen of the sky appeared unusually far away and touchable at the same time. One could have heard a pin drop at two miles. There was no wind, no sound, and only the faintest odor of something like dryness, and I thought of the sand.

Feelings flooded me, peeved and mystified by E.J.'s fear—how was it possible I'd married a man afraid of the dark?—while awed by the bigness of the sky, the sharpness of the stars. And I had creepy-flesh. I couldn't understand it. Was E.J.'s fear contagious?

Something about the poised, heavy stillness hung about us, as if a gigantic being had taken a step and was just about to put the other foot down when we came out of our tent—as if that huge, unseeable foot hovered, waiting for us to return to our tent so it could continue its restless night meandering.

We walked back to the tent, still not speaking, but the moment we got inside, I made E.J. pull his cot up alongside mine and talk to me.

"Didn't you feel anything out there?" he asked.

"You mean, besides the beauty and the peace and the quiet?"

"Beauty and quiet, yes. Peace, no. The night belongs to creatures of the dark, especially in this part of the world. Didn't you feel like someone or something was waiting for us to get out of its way?"

I refused to add fuel to the fire of his fantasy. "For heaven's sake, why did you go into archeology if you believe in this stuff?"

"Because I have to take on the fear, although I didn't think I'd have to face it so soon. I have to find out about the Djinneyah, and arm myself against...."

"Who?"

"Beings created of smokeless fire."

"That's Islamic myth, E.J., I thought you were Christian." Now *I* began to feel fear. Never mind folkloric Djinneyah, I had married a real live mad man.

"I've seen Djinneyah. Or *not* seen her."

"Uh-huh," I tried to sound agreeable. "Well, I've not seen her either—too."

"I was twelve," he went on, "when my friends dared me to walk on an ancient road that was a trade-route before the time of Christ at a bit of a distance from our village. At that time, I feared nothing. My pragmatic parents didn't believe in supernatural forces, and that's how I was socialized. I went to the spot where folklore says she's stolen men for millennia. She's particularly fond of men. I felt spooky, but I wasn't frightened.

"Then the Djinneyah came. I remember noise and odors and I remember her yelling, 'this is just a boy! But he will make a good man for me one day.' My eyes used to be hazel, before that night. She marked me by taking the color from my eyes."

"My folklore is a bit rusty," I argued as I fell back to sleep, "but isn't it impossible for a mere mortal to take on the disembodied dark forces?"

"Not impossible, no. There's tremendous power in being physical. We're dense matter, which Djinneyah loves to consume, but she can't if you're not afraid. Fear is vulnerability, and vulnerability is an open door to the spark of life."

"Can't wait to hear more..." I mumbled, tumbling back into sleep. I'd be lying if I said I had no dreams.

* *

When I woke in the morning, E.J. was already a member of the breakfast-making crew. He kissed my forehead as if no weirdness had transpired between us in the night.

Everyone raved about his pancakes. Everyone liked him. He was the translator, made great pancakes, and was a nice guy. There wasn't anyone I could walk up to and say, "excuse me, but last night I discovered I've married a mad man."

Blythe Ayne – 7

The whole crew struggled to stay awake so that the following day we'd be more or less on local time. The pay-off was that E.J. stayed asleep through the night, and so did I.

But the first night's events lingered, and by the third day I couldn't stand the suspense and the confused feelings about my new husband. As I brushed my hair, I dared to bring up the subject. "E.J., about this Djinneyah thing—am I right in guessing that you came here—on this dig—to face it?"

He sat on the edge of his cot, watching me brushing my hair with fascination. "Before we left the states, yes. But now it seems enough just to be here and to do the work I'm doing."

I nodded. "You must know that I don't believe in any of that stuff. Not only that, but I'm wondering how you expect to lead a scientific life if you do believe in it? I love folklore, but it's just stories."

E.J. shrugged, but had nothing further to say, and I let it drop. Well, I thought, maybe my pragmatic beliefs would bring him back to reality.

So he shocked my once again when, the next evening after supper as we were walking back to our cozy tent he said, "I've arranged to borrow one of the jeeps tonight."

"Really? Why?"

"To meet the Djinneyah. You've shown me these last couple days that you'll never respect me again, that we'll never be close again, unless I prove her existence to you."

I hadn't realized how much his nonsense had tempered my feelings for him, nor how obvious my changed feelings were. But he was absolutely correct.

Anyway, I thought the jeep ride in the velvety evening a great idea. And I was equally determined that E.J.

see the Djinneyah's nonexistence. I kept that thought to myself.

We drove almost an hour on the hard-packed, rib-crunching dirt road. The sun sat on the great straight line of horizon directly behind us and, as much as I wanted to feel like I was on an adventure, a lark, there was an uncomfortable silence between us. I wondered what E.J. would do when no Djinneyah materialized.

We came to scrubby vegetation along the roadside. E.J. suddenly turned the headlights and the engine off and steered the jeep off the road. With the sun now gone, night wrapped around us as if we'd been shoved into a black closet. E.J. coasted around behind the scrub. I heard him get out and walk around to my side of the jeep. Silently, he took my hand and led me into the scrub.

He pulled me to the ground. My eyes were becoming adjusted to the dark—I could make out the shape of the scraggly bushes around us, I could see the stars, the hard-packed blackness of the road, the outline of E.J.'s body, stretched on the ground. A ragged edge of moon came into the sky with a wobbly, flickering light. Even the wan moonlight made everything stand out in dramatic bas-relief.

Then something stirred—an odd swirl of wind curled around us, laced with the redolence of cardamom. I breathed deeply, heady and dizzy with the fragrance on the breeze. The night colors distinguished themselves—the zaffer blue sand, the purple sky, the ebony branches and black bisque leaves of the scrub, and E.J.'s pale hair, pale eyes glowing with a silver-blue hue.

How strange he looked!

That was when the raucous noise began. Coming toward us on the road were the sounds of a band of

Gypsies—tribal entertainment. It was the tambourines I heard first, accompanied by the high piercing tinkle of ankle bells. Then laughter—cheerful, infectious. A donkey brayed, answered by two or three others. A drum beat pounded with a deep-to-the-feet thrum. Soon the nye and muzmar joined in with a provocative melody.

A camel coughed and another bellowed out over the flat land. Several voices raised in song, while a child's giggle could be heard above the urgent melody.

What luck! I thought, what a coincidence, to come to *nowhere* in the middle of the night, to lie prostrate on the earth for no reason, and to be treated to a wandering band of Gypsies. I couldn't wait to see their bright, swirling fabrics, the gaudily dressed donkeys and camels, the madly painted homes on wheels, the dark eyes and gold jewelry and long black hair.

I jumped up in anticipation. E.J. reached for me quick as a snake and slammed me back to the ground.

"What's the matter with you?" I snarled.

"What's the matter with *you*," he whispered back, not letting go of my arm.

Then I had second thoughts. This was his homeland, he surely knew more about it than I. A band of Gypsies on an abandoned road in the middle of the night—they'd probably steal me and sell me into white slavery.

"Are the Gypsies dangerous?"

"Gypsies?" E.J. hissed. "It's not Gypsies, it's the Djinneyah and her demons."

"Still with the Djinneyah thing!" I hissed back. Then I stopped whispering. "For God's sake, Elias, give it a rest!" I shouted, angry beyond reason.

All the myriad sounds of the oncoming troupe stopped instantly—a metronome count of four—then started up again. I wrenched myself from E.J.'s grasp, stood and stumbled away from him. Pushing aside the brush, I peered at the road.

From the sounds, the troupe must have been fast upon me, but I saw nothing. I glanced at E.J. to see if he'd try to grab at me again, but he was cowering in the sand, looking frightened to death. I found myself feeling intense disgust for such a paltry excuse of a man.

The singing drew my attention back to the road. What melody, what sound! Could any human voice produce such clarion perfection? I fell in love with the song, the sound of that music, that singing, those drums, as if altogether it was a creature I longed to hold. The music was right *there* as I stared at the road, glowing black in the wilted moonlight. Where were they?

Then I saw the sharp-edged print of hooves appear in the dirt road and long thin trails, the marks of wagon wheels. The singing and the tambourines and the ankle bells were directly before me, but there was nothing other than the legion of hoof and wheel prints materializing before my eyes.

The music augmented in volume and intensity as the nye and muzmar and the big drum passed directly in front of me, with only more prints appearing in the sand. I couldn't stand it! I stepped through the brush onto the road, right into the arms of a tall, beautiful, amber-eyed woman. She smiled and I saw that her teeth were too large, quite literally looking like pearls. She began to speak, but, even though her mouth moved, the sound of her voice came from the night and from the earth. She spoke in a pre-Koranic Arabic, and yet I understood every word, although I marginally knew modern Arabic.

"I'm pleased by your appreciation of my music," she said, "and it's good that you please me. It's also good that you bring Elias back to me now that he is a man." The red of her cloak swirled around me like an alien dawn. "Since you've pleased me, I will not make of you a bodiless creature, haunting the desert until the end of time. I'll simply take your mortal life."

E.J. came flying through the brush as if he'd become a demon himself. I was unaware that the Djinneyah had folded me to her, but when E.J. flung her cloak away from me, I tripped backwards and sat flat on the ground.

Like a child I watched.

"Withdraw yourself from my beloved and from me!" E.J. commanded with a frightening authority in that ancient language. "In the name of the Lord of the Mystery of Heaven and Earth, the Lord of the Two Easts and the Two Wests, the Lord of Dawn, I command you! Remove your impudent and evil spirit, and all your attending consorts and legions." His body shook with fury and his voice cut through the din of the unseen like a lighthouse beam.

The music swelled and wailed, the Djinneyah's laughter poured from every grain of sand, every leaf, every branch, the odor of burning rose water built to a crescendo with the music. Then, instantly, it was gone. As the Djinneyah disappeared in a swirl of red, my eyes were drawn to her two furry black fetlocks and shiny black hooves that were before me and then were gone.

All that remained were the prints of the mad trampling of cloven feet.

E.J. pulled me up from the dirt, dusted me off, put his arm around me, and walked me back to the jeep. I held onto him all the way back to the camp, without uttering a word.

*   *

The most interesting thing about life is not the things that happen in it, as much as what one learns from living through it. Although that night was amazing, and although I came to believe in things I previously couldn't have imagined, nothing made a greater impression on me than seeing how much my husband loved me. More than I loved him. More than he loved himself. That's when I began to truly love my now hazel-eyed husband. I learned to love how he's different from me even more than how he's the same.

And this is the wisdom I intend to pass on to our children.

END

Last Request

I'm at the *Health & Welfare* office—that's what they call it, but there's little health here. Lots of welfare, but little health.

I see my reflection in the front windows, the broken shades have been partially pulled letting in broken shards of light. As much as I'd rather not see my reflection, I do. It's even more broken than the window shades, the shards of light. I remember my former self, a big, buff, football coach. Now, here's this shattered reflection—a reflection of a reflection.

There's a bunch of people playing monopoly, waiting for their names to be called, waiting to get their share of health and welfare. As if either can simply be doled out.

Someone behind me says, "Can you do one thing for me?"

I turn. There stands the most beautiful woman I've ever seen this side of paradise.

Just like in the movies, I look around me to see who she's addressing.

And I say, "Are you talking to me?"

She doesn't move or say anything.

"Are you talking to me?"

"I can tell," she says, "you're a gentle soul. Can you do one thing for me?"

"I ... I don't know." No one has asked me to do anything for them since the cancer got my guts and my wife couldn't stand to watch me fade away and she, mercifully for both of us, left me.

"I used to do things for people every day. But ...."

"I know," she says, since you got sick."

"That's right." I can't help staring. Her big violet eyes remind me of something, and I can't look away. I see a tear course down her cheek. "What, my dear, what? If I can help, I will. But ...."

"My son needs me, but I can't reach him."

"Why not?"

"I got so sick, and I couldn't stay. I had to leave. Didn't want to. But ... just ... couldn't hang on."

I'm utterly confused. "So you want me to?...."

"I want you to find him and take care of him."

"Me? Oh, I believe you'd better find someone else."

"There's not one else here." Her sad voice rolls around in my cavernous disease-infested chest.

All around me, the place is jam-packed with people. But ... funny thing, as my eyes pass over the window where I see my reflection, the beautiful woman isn't standing beside me.

I turn to her. She reads my thought.

"Where are you? *What* are you?" I ask.

"I'm here and not here. Between worlds—because of my son. Unfinished business."

I look up at the *Health & Welfare* sign, contemplating my remaining short journey.

"What kind of power do you have to appear to me, to talk to me?"

"I don't know … I've been looking for a kind person, who has the same fractal pattern as my son."

The same fractal pattern? "What?"

"Oh, too difficult to explain. But … when you … that is … eventually it'll be perfectly clear."

"Never mind." I look deep into her violet eyes. "Can you trade places with me?"

"Truly?" she asks, shocked.

"Truly. I don't have much time here, it really doesn't make much difference to me. You won't have long, but it's better than leaving unfinished business."

In a flash, I find myself inside a fractal pattern, looking through it at the most beautiful woman I'd ever seen, though obviously in poor health, walking out of the *Health & Welfare* office, with a huge smile on her face.

It fills me with joy as I turn, peering down this new path. I hurry toward a wonderful light at the end of a swirling fractal tunnel.

END

Lila
By award winning author
Blythe Ayne
A short story

First Position

Rain thrummed against the old wooden platform of the train station. The water standing on the shiny black surface of the wood quivered. Lila felt shock waves through her soft white boots as Amtrak's silver engine shot out of the blackness across the trestle and into the feeble yellow light of the station, then stopped, purring.

She grabbed the handles of her valise, stepped through the unpainted, unvarnished wooden door of the time-forgotten train station, opened her umbrella and tiptoed across the loose pebbles to the conductor, who stood by the two steps up into the train, waiting to give her a hand. He stomped from foot to foot, making it clear he had no affection for standing in the rain a moment longer than necessary for the sake of one passenger.

Lila handed him her ticket, closed her umbrella and stepped onto the train.

"What a night!" the conductor said, stepping on behind her.

"Yes." Lila didn't turn to look at him. "Quite." She made her way down the length of the car. It was not entirely full, but too crowded for her comfort. She could remember a time when she would have settled herself between the two boisterous families—safety in numbers. But now she wanted quiet. Peace. Privacy.

She went through three cars and finally came to one that was completely empty. She settled at the far end, returning to her reverie.

As the wet night hurried by the dark glass of the window, Lila studied her dark, dramatically changed, reflection. Her cameo skin was as flawless as a re-touched photograph, and ever since she'd gotten over the hyperthyroid problem, her hair had grown long—luxuriant, shining blonde, paler than corn silk. Its natural curl had returned, cascading to the small of her back in perfect waves.

The soft blue of her eyes reflected back a shade darker. Her cheekbones appeared more pronounced and her eyes larger than she remembered. Was it the dark-glass reflection? Was it the change in her health? Was it the change in what she wore, or how she now carried herself? The lacy white collar encircling her throat suited her better than the T-shirts she used to wear.

Most probably, she thought, her striking physical changes were due to the even more profound spiritual changes. Perhaps, she reprimanded herself, she ought not have these vain thoughts about her physicality, when her new spirituality was all that mattered. On the other hand, these thoughts didn't feel anything like the worrisome, critical ones she'd had about herself, her appearance, before her conversion.

The train slowed, then chuffed to a stop at yet another berg perched alongside the railroad tracks. Lila watched a young mother with three small children hurry to the train, followed by a tall, lean man.

Looking up, he caught Lila's glance. His black eyes held her gaze for a moment, his complexion a whiteness almost whiter than Lila's own. He appeared to glow in the shroud of rain and night. He stepped onto the train.

Then out from the train station scurried a rotund little man, smiling and harried all at once, who seemed more likely to be the husband and father of the family that had already clambered aboard than the other, arresting, man.

Lila listened as the noise of the family approached, hoping they'd not invade her privacy. The jabbering children and the high-pitched voice of their mother, came through to the neighboring car and stopped, the brood apparently roosting there as the train moved forward.

Lila relaxed and closed her eyes, following some thought knocking around in her mind. She let the sound and the sensation of the train's motion, *ta-dum, ta-dum,* pour into her, conjuring up old memories. Something about that rhythm connected her to another time.

A reminiscence she'd completely forgotten began to unfold. She saw herself as a small child with her mother, on a train. It was cold. Bitter, winter, cold. Lila recalled looking up into her mother's eyes, and seeing great sadness. She was cold, though her mother held her close, wrapped in a blanket—she must have been an infant. What a terrible feeling, that cold! Her mother had been visiting her mother.

Lila could just barely remember a sensation of perfect coziness, between her mother and her grandmother, taking turns holding her as if neither of them could possibly get enough, sitting close together before a dancing fire.

And then, the memory that triggered the others, of her mother, unhappy and lonely as she returned to Lila's father. The train was cold, and her mother sad, which had made Lila feel cold.

Amazing! Lila thought. What I knew as an infant—that Mother was missing her mother, and knowing that, made me cold. I never realized how much I despise cold until this moment, with that memory. That was why ....

She felt someone looking at her. Her eyes flew open. Across from her sat the pale man who had gotten on at the last station. Everything about him, other than his disconcertingly glowing white skin, was black—black hair, combed back with an errant lock falling onto his forehead. Intense black eyebrows over black, heavily-lashed eyes. Black turtle neck sweater, black top coat, black slacks, sox, shoes. An onyx weighted the slender ring finger of his right hand.

"Meditating?" He ran his fingers through his damp hair, openly studying her.

She nodded. "Are there no other vacant seats?" she asked pointedly.

He laughed and leaned toward her, as if there was any reason at all to be familiar. Lila noted a musty scent from him. "I make it my habit, when opportunity presents, to sit with a beautiful woman in view. And here you are. By far the most beautiful woman on this train. Or in some surrounding distance, I would dare to wager."

"But I want to sit alone." Lila answered, unblinking. What amazing strength she had since her conversion! She could never have been so incisive nor outspoken before. She would have suffered in silence.

"Oh, come now, you don't mean that." He settled more comfortably into the seat.

Why did he feel he had the right to impose himself on her? She'd been perfectly clear. She studied him for a moment and noticed, finally, that he was very good looking. Women most surely never told him "no." And even if they did, as she just had, he wouldn't hear it.

Strange and interesting—he seemed to exude coldness, right on the heels of her introspection about cold. Only her curiosity regarding this uncanny coincidence kept her from moving to another seat.

Second Position

"On your way to Seattle?" He flashed a smile full of large, white teeth.

"Yes."

"By the way, I'm Renwick. Ren, for short." He extended his hand.

"Where the raven's live." Lila refrained from taking his hand.

His smile broadened. "Amazing! No one ever knows that."

Lila shrugged.

Ren saw that Lila didn't intend to take his hand and he let it drop to his lap. "I'm beginning to think you don't like me."

"What were the clues?" Lila shocked herself yet more. She'd never been sarcastic!

Ren narrowed his eyes—Lila felt his anger. Then a calmness came over his face. "I wonder what some man did to get you to hate *all* men so." His black eyes pulled at her. "Don't you believe in love?"

She looked out the rain-streaked window at the maelstrom of night and stormy elements, a mere pane of glass away. Little silver daggers of rain slammed against the window, begging, cajoling, to be let in. The wind sighing, the rain crying, "let us in, let us become warm, and still, and dry."

She turned to the stranger and looked into him to see his picture of love. "What you call ... love ... I remember the effect it had on me. I gave myself up to the whimsy of it. In return for my self-sacrifice, I was beaten, abused, cheated on, belittled, ignored." She paused like she might go on. But she didn't. She had no desire, no need, to look at those pictures now.

Ren's cold eyes had warmed, although they still harbored a dispassionate glint. "You just ... attracted the wrong kind of man—were attracted to the wrong ...."

Lila interrupted him. "Now that you've solved my problems, at least in your world view, I'd very much appreciate it if you would kindly move to another seat." She felt impassive, not even angry, really. But annoyed, yes. Somewhat annoyed.

She sensed the frustrated anger rising in this man again. "If you've excised men from your life, you shouldn't be so beautiful."

"It's my business what I look like." Lila picked up her valise, umbrella and coat, and stood. "And none of yours."

Ren stood and put his hand on her forearm. "I'll leave. I thought we were sparring, maybe even flirting. But I see you really do want me to move." He stepped into the aisle and walked away.

Lila didn't bother to watch him leave. She settled herself again and wondered at his ability to annoy her. Even if this was her first time out alone, she thought the rigorous discipline she'd been taught about emotions assured that she had complete power over her own.

She had much to learn.

Returning to her self-observations she realized that before her conversion, she would have *swooned* over Ren. Now she felt almost nothing. She decided it was the surging rhythm of the train, the rhythmic pulsing, passing through her body, that caught her up in her emotions. And his. There was, too, that musky scent emanating from him, which she'd first found unlikable. When he stood beside her, when he touched her forearm, it had changed, briefly, from unlikable to attractive.

Strange.

Now, alone with her thoughts, she contemplated her journey, soon to arrive in Seattle, returning to ballet. But this time with both her physical and mental health. She took comfort in the knowledge that she was cared for, *eternally.* She had put the concerns of the flesh behind her, and celebrated eternity. She smiled to herself, at the precise moment Ren walked by.

Third Position

He glanced at her, and, taking in her smile, he paused. "A penny for your thoughts."

"My thoughts are worth considerably more."

"Without a doubt. I'd give considerably more just to know your name."

"Lila."

"Lila. Yes, Perfect. Lovely Lila. So. Lila, let me guess, your life has something to do with music ...."

"Yes."

"You're a dancer."

"Yes."

Ren remained in the aisle, swaying with the train's motion.

"How did you put that together?" she asked.

"First, I see you've taken your shoes off, even though it's chilly. In my experience, dancers are forever kicking their shoes off. Second, you carry yourself like a dancer.

And third, you look like a dancer." He flashed his toothsome smile.

Carnivorous, Lila thought, attractive, but carnivorous.

"I was just heading to the dining car," he continued. "Would you care to join me? I'll buy you, well, whatever passes for dinner on this train."

Lila thought, with distaste, of watching him ingest a fat steak. "No, thanks."

"I'm not hungry myself, I just thought I'd have some tea or a glass of wine. Something to warm me up. This train is inexcusably cold."

"I don't ...." It suddenly came to Lila that Ren was almost certainly one of the tests she'd been told she'd face, to cope with living in ordinary human society again. "Well, why not?"

She put her feet in her delicate boots and pulled her white coat over her shoulders.

They walked through to the dining car, Ren solicitously taking her elbow at the slightest lurch. Oddly, his muskiness intrigued her yet more, enigmatic and stirring some not-yet-revealed insight. Her sleeping emotions awakened—she felt confused, annoyed, delighted.

And *somehow* it was tied to the pulsing motion of the train. The *ta-dum, ta-dum,* the sound and gentle sway over the tracks stirred her deeply. Sensuously.

Oh! She didn't need that! But if it was in her, she must learn to understand it.

"What would you like?" Ren asked after they were seated and the waiter handed them menus.

Lila glanced at the menu, but her mind was on Ren. How had he gone from unattractive to attractive, from insensitive to sensitive, from boring to intriguing, so rapidly?

"I'm not hungry—exactly. I … I'll have a green salad, no dressing."

Ren glanced at the waiter and he came up to them.

"Yes sir?"

"The lady will have a green salad sans dressing, and kindly bring us a carafe of burgundy with two glasses."

"What kind of dressing, sir?"

"Without dressing."

"Very good."

When the waiter was out of ear shot, they looked at one another and giggled. "Sans dressing," Ren said. "Very exotic, all the rage."

Lila couldn't believe such a silly thing would make her laugh. Oddity after oddity! The confusion unnerved her. She felt through her lacy collar to the golden icon clasped around her throat. He cannot harm me, she silently recited.

"What's wrong?"

Lila put her hand in her lap. "Nothing. Just … nervous habit."

"There's nothing to be nervous about."

"I know."

The waiter brought the wine and salad.

"To your health," Ren toasted.

"And to yours." Lila sipped cautiously. How long since she'd tasted wine?

"So," Ren continued, "I'm going to Seattle too, thanks for asking. Going to vacation with some musician friends. Kind of an underground bunch, but you never know when someone's going to make it big. Do you have a place to stay when you get there?"

"Of course."

"Of course." He nodded. "Well, your turn."

"My turn?"

"To make conversation."

"I don't feel obligated to make conversation, you're the one who's latched onto me."

"True, but ....." he paused. "You've been away from people, haven't you? Out of the mainstream, away small talk, away from small social norms. Away from realizing that your beauty, your self-assurance, will attract attention."

Fourth Position

At that moment, one of the family broods came into the dining car. Four children, mother and father, all bleary-eyed and noisy.

"Chocolate shakes, all around," the father ordered.

"I want strawberry!" a smaller child cried.

They looked like peas in a pod—brown hair, pale eyes, freckles. Even the mother and father looked enough alike to be first cousins.

The oldest girl had glued her attention onto Lila and Ren. She elbowed her mother and pointed her nose in their direction. Mom, with an entrenched worry frown, caught Lila's glance, then made a small, embarrassed gasp and looked down. "It's not polite to stare, Mary Sue," she whispered.

"But they're so *beauuu-ti-ful!*" Mary Sue stage whispered.

"Do you want to leave?" Ren poured the last of the wine into their glasses. "You haven't touched your salad, but our peace is disrupted."

"No, I'll stay." Lila had become fascinated with the organized chaos of the family. Like an organism of its own making, every move appeared virtually choreographed. Each one of them knew what the others were about to do, and even though the children squabbled, while the parents added as much to the confusion by continually begging for quiet, there was enough electrical current of affection among them, Lila thought, to light a village.

They smelled like the fresh outdoors. They must make their lives on the farm, she surmised.

"Waiter?" the mother called.

"Yes, ma'am?"

"How long until we stop at Lacey?"

"Approximately half an hour."

"Hear that kids? We've only got thirty minutes to home."

"*YAY!*" the children roared.

"He said half-an-hour," the littlest boy protested.

"Same thing. Now get that milk shake in you." The mother turned to the waiter. "We've been to Portland visiting relatives. The train's a great way to go. I love the train!"

"Shoulda flown, be home by now," the father groused quietly.

"Hon! That's not polite. Not true, either, by the time you drive to and from airports."

Ren leaned toward Lila. "Why so fascinated?" he whispered.

"They're so—*together*. Completely in tune with each other."

Ren nodded. "You want children?"

"No children!" Lila took one last glance at the family, stood and left the dining car, Ren following.

"What ...." he held the doors open for her as they passed between the cars. "Why are you upset?"

"I ...." She paused, studying her emotions. "I'm not upset. No. I simply need to be quiet. And alone. I'm not ... not ready to interact with a stranger to this degree. You're too familiar with me." She stood by her seat refusing to sit, wanting Ren to leave her alone. Something stirred in her, something strange and new, something unbidden. She desperately, urgently, needed to be left alone.

"But I want to get to know you. I want to not be a stranger to you." He dared to put his hand on her shoulder. "I want to know what happened to you that makes you so closed off. So afraid."

"You misunderstand. I'm not afraid." She tolerated his touch, with irritation and curiosity.

He shook his head. "What did they do to you—whoever 'they' are?"

"'They' gave me so much. None of which you'd understand. Before they saved me, my life was a disaster. Everyone I loved died, I was abused by people I trusted, my health was tail-spinning. The night I despaired of any reason to continue living, they found me and took me to the cloister. There I was made whole in body, mind, and, most importantly, spirit."

"But," Ren whispered in her ear, "someone could care for you without being a religious fanatic."

"I didn't say they were religious fanatics."

"You didn't have to. I could make you happy, Lila." He inclined his face close to her, his whiter-than-white skin and his huge white teeth coming toward her.

Fifth Position

"No!" Lila whispered. She snapped her fingers, the lights went out. She sank her fangs into his jugular, his musky scent of mortality rose up around and through her.

"*Oh!*" Ren exclaimed quietly.

Retiré

When the train pulled into the station, Lila stood by the door, valise and umbrella in hand. The rain had stopped.

It was much as they had said her first time alone would be. Fighting it, then giving in. She'd left enough mortality in Ren that he would search high and low for her. Which would serve her well when he offered her dinner again.

The instant the train stopped, all was still in her. The heartbeat, the *ta-dum, ta-dum* of the train had confused her, made her recall escaped memories. There was a time when she'd had a fragile, delicate, beating heart, like everyone else.

But she'd forgotten the sensation, the mortal longings, arising from the incessant rhythm, reminding her of cold, of warmth, of a mother, of human love. Of all that her life had been when mortal.

Poor health, heartbreak, abuse—all, *all* forgotten without the beat of a heart. That was why they'd insisted she take the train.

The only longing she never lost was her love of dance. Her teachers told her that if she insisted on returning to the world of mortals, she couldn't let rhythms—of trains, of ocean waves, of music, of the breath of mortals, of *anything*—distract her from her art.

The dance. The dance was everything.

Lila pulled her coat close around her and stepped from the train.

END

Believe This!

"**Y**eah, I can believe that," the lanky delivery guy said as he plopped a pile of cartons marked "FRAGILE" in big, red, block letters down on the floor—fragile ceramics and pottery I'd been waiting and waiting and waiting for, for weeks.

I tore my eyes away from the pile of undoubtedly shattered artifacts and looked at him. "What?"

"Yeah," he said, grinning. Cute in a vapid, scruffy, self-centered way. He put his hand to his Bluetooth to let me know he had something more important than either me or my delivery taking his attention. "I can believe that."

He held out his signature box for me to scribble an electronic signature. At that moment, the top carton teetered and fell to the floor.

"Whoops!" he said. Then chuckled. "Yeah, I can believe that. No shit, yeah."

Although he'd been looking at me, he hadn't really been looking at me—it was that sort of defocused stare people have when they're hypnotized or sleep walking. Now he focused.

"Hey," he said, "I think I gotta go—I'll get back to ya." He shoved the box at me again. "Signature, please." He strained to be polite. He had the energy of a big, tail-wagging dog in grandma's knick-knack-filled parlor. I wanted him gone as much as he did.

"Are you aware of having dropped valuable art objects on the floor?" My heart pounded. Nothing, nothing, *nothing* makes me more miserable than confrontation.

He shrugged. "They're okay."

"I've called your office about this delivery six times!"

"Yeah. I can believe that. But I gotta have your signature—I got a lot of deliveries. Have a heart."

"You're not going anywhere before I open these cartons." I engaged my, "I mean business" voice to its limits. It didn't even convince me.

I went to the back and got a box cutter. As I returned, the sun, slanting through the window, shot through the new art glass that came in yesterday—its deep indigo blues and wild oranges cast fingers of bold light across the art gallery. How I loved this place! Even though I'd given up a fantastic, fairly secure career as a graphic designer in a big prepress firm for the risky business of opening my own gallery, it was worth it every second of every day.

I opened the first carton—the one that fell to the floor. With the opening of the carton exhaled the heady fragrance of plumeria. I carefully pulled out a gorgeous terra cotta Pele. Perfectly intact. Amazing—she ought to have been shattered.

Carton after carton I drew out a stunning array of goddesses, each more beautiful and powerful than the previous. Each carton I slit open released an exotic fragrance from places as far flung as the goddess figurines themselves—not a chip on a single one. *Miraculous!*

Back on his phone, the delivery guy fidgeted around the gallery, prowling back and forth in the indigo and orange light, barely tolerating my careful examination of each artifact. I despised his nervous energy thrashing among the delicate art, and longed for him to shut up and stop moving.

"Yeah, I can believe that," he said, yet again.

What a dufus! I came to the last carton. Opening it carefully, I beheld a blue glaze Kali. The aroma accompanying her was *not* sweet. It was sulfuric. Strange to say, that scent matched my feelings. At fourteen inches, she stood the tallest of the array of little goddesses. Her terrifying beauty in full wrathful stance, one foot on a skull, her other foot raised as if to step right out of the carton.

And, in fact, that's what she did.

She stepped out onto the floor, while the other goddesses gathered behind her. They moved toward the delivery guy who stood with his back to us, still jabbering away on his phone. As they moved, the beautiful indigo and orange light filtering through the art glass ran together, flowing into molten browns and grays right before my eyes—and the delivery guy's eyes too, but his self-absorption kept him oblivious.

The goddesses flew upon him with strange and lightning speed. He yelled inarticulately, batting at them, his Bluetooth dislodged and slammed into the wall across the room.

I stood, grounded to the spot, bewitched.

Kali wrested the signature box from his hand, jumped on his shoulder and smacked him on the head until he slumped into unconsciousness.

"*Believe that!*" she said with unvarnished disgust. Aghast as I was at the violence, I experienced a weird, calm satisfaction.

The goddesses returned to where I'd first set them and resumed their ceramic state, while the indigo and orange light flowed over the lanky delivery guy, finally quiet at last.

END

Gift in the Night

Night had fallen with a thud, which still unnerved Hope. It was only her second winter in Portland, and she was not yet adjusted to the cloud-covered twilight at four-thirty in the afternoon. She doubted she ever would.

As she drove around trying to find an old movie theatre having a Black & White Film Revival, she'd become lost among the mazy streets. She'd missed the beginning of the first show and didn't feel like waiting around for the second, even if she did manage to find the theatre. Her back was so frozen up with pain from the tension of being lost, she knew she couldn't sit through a movie anyway.

She decided to park and walk around—try to relax some of the seized muscles. Besides, she suddenly noticed, she was surrounded by enchanting shops with pale lights filtering through small, smuchy windows.

Hope wrangled her car into a parallel parking spot, turned off the engine. She pulled herself out of the car, then clutched the back of her neck with one hand and her lumbar vertebrae with the other. That parallel parking really took it out of her. She breathed deeply and thought about "being relaxed." Then she looked around.

The little shops that had attracted her were all identified with the talismanic filigree of Chinese writing. Hope glanced in the windows of the shops as she wandered by, catching sight and spicy redolence of fowls denuded of feathers but otherwise intact hanging from the rafters like winter vegetables, a gift shop with gaudy toys next to risque adult nicknacks, and racks of post cards of Portland's skyline and The Great Wall of China. She passed a little restaurant with strings of brightly painted paper lanterns threaded low overhead.

Inside each shop a shopkeeper sat chatting with customers. Everyone leaned their elbows on glass showcases, gazing out at the sidewalk. Hope sensed she was more of a curiosity to the locals than their shops were to her. At five-foot-ten, with pale white skin, long, wavy brown hair, and big, round blue eyes, she didn't exactly blend in.

She crossed the street and passed a martial arts studio with a class in full, bone-crunching motion. Hope winced as, en masse, half the class threw the other half to the floor. Just seeing it made cat-claws of pain climb up her back. She hurried to the corner, paying no attention to the shops she passed. She didn't even want to hear those bodies thumping to the floor again.

When next she looked around, she found herself standing by a large storefront window with the word "Pharmacy" printed in pale green block lettering on the clean glass, with, again, the lilting, delicate lines of some entirely arcane to her Chinese writing beneath it.

Peering through the window, Hope saw walls lined from knee-level to ceiling with giant apothecary jars. Her eyes roved over the rows and rows of tall, clear glass jars with rounded glass lids and their mysterious contents.

Then she noticed the thin, elderly Chinese man, perched on a stool behind a high counter, his head very nearly the same size and shape as the uniform jars. Long silver hair framed his long thin, pale parchment-like face, with his keen, deep-set eyes fixed on Hope while she gazed at the jars like an astronomer discovering a galaxy.

Self consciously lowering her eyes, she hurried to the end of the block and teetered on the edge of the curb, trying to decide whether to go home, or continue her window shopping, which felt like part voyeurism and part exhibitionism.

Just as the light changed, insight struck. "Sometimes, Hope, you're downright slow!" she told herself. "Here you are, suffering from an incessant pain that no physical therapist, or surgeon, or medication has been able to improve, and you walk right by what might be a gift in the night."

She returned to the pharmacy and pushed through the jangling door. Ginseng languished redolently on the air, mixed with other aromas she'd never smelled. The Chinese man, thin as paper, stood up from his stool, remained almost exactly the same height as when seated.

He studied her with disconcerting directness.

"Ahhm ...." Hope wondered if he spoke English. "Pharmacy" was the only English word she'd seen.

"You have back problem," he said. He pointed to his neck and then his lower back. "Up, and down."

"Why, yes. How ... how do you know?"

He made a large wavery gesture with both hands around her. "Body gives light. Spine-light sad. Weak up, and down."

"Yes." Hope nodded. "And makes me sad too."

"Sure!"

"I wonder if you have anything I could try that would, maybe, reduce the pain, but won't knock me out or make me feel stupid."

"Sure, sure!" he said, pulling apothecary jars from shelves, grinding, mashing, sieving, who-knew-what together, then, quick as elves' hands, pouring the concoction into capsules and funneling them into a dark brown glass bottle. He stuck a cork in the top and a label on the side. He bent over the label with a pen and scratched away for a few moments.

Hope, mesmerized by his spare movements as rhythmic as a percussion artist, wondered anxiously what he had concocted and how she would possibly be able to pay him. All the doctors with all their medication had strapped her financially, plus her system had become disconcertingly sensitive to just about every kind of drug.

The Chinese pharmacist put the bottle in a sack and handed it to her.

"Ah, well, ah, how much does this cost?"

"Seven dollars."

"Seven dollars? Just—seven dollars?" Hope couldn't believe it, it had been worth seven dollars to watch his ancient-yet-smooth hands perform.

"You can give me more," he laughed, *tee-hee*, "but I think you don't have it. My job is to make body whole. Money is just so you believe."

"Oh." Hope nodded. She understood what he said, but she couldn't believe that's what he meant to say.

"So, what's in this?" She rattled the sack.

"Natural herbs, natural things. Best medicine."

"And when do I take them?"

"Instructions on the bottle." He mimed scribing in the air. "That's why I write on label. You take one three times a day."

"And they'll help my pain, but not put me to sleep?"

"Sure, sure. Don't worry—*believe*. Medicine has no side effect. It will stop pain tomorrow at this time, if you take one tonight, two tomorrow. New, fresh blood will go, quick, hurry, to bad places in back. You will heal. No more bad back."

"Oh, I don't know, I've got injured discs and vertebrae. They don't get better, I just don't want to get worse. And I hope to find *something* that will subdue the pain."

The Chinese man nodded to everything she said, but when she stopped talking he said, "No! You must want bigger. New blood with special herbs to heal back. Sure, sure. Believe it."

"Well, okay." Hope paid him then grabbed up his business card with English on one side and Chinese on the other. It didn't seem polite to argue with someone who appeared to truly believe that healing was his only objective. And maybe, she thought, it wouldn't hurt her to try and believe again, too.

She used to believe in getting better. But so many doctors and physical therapists had told her she wouldn't, that she'd finally conceded to them.

*   *

Hope found herself pulling into her carport. She looked around, bewildered. She couldn't even remember getting in her car, let alone finding her way out of the maze of neighborhood streets and back onto the thoroughfare, then to her own side streets.

She grabbed the little sack and hurried inside. In the kitchen she took the brown-glass bottle out of its sack and looked at the label, half expecting it to not be in English, or not be legible. Instead, in a delicate English cursive was written, "Take one capsule every eight hours."

*   *

A few days later, Hope's physical therapist commented on how relaxed her muscles seemed, and a couple days after that, her neurosurgeon noted that she had a wider range of movement. One said it was probably because it hadn't been raining for the last few days, the other observed that the new medication he'd prescribed must be letting her sleep better.

Hope said, "um-hum" to one and "I see" to the other. But she kept the real reason to herself. She knew it wasn't in either of *their* best interests for her to have discovered a miracle.

The next week she skipped a couple therapy appointments and the week after that, without explanation to anyone, she quit going altogether. They wouldn't accept it if she simply told them, "I'm healed!" And much worse than that, they would try to convince her that *she* must not accept such a ridiculous notion.

Hope didn't want anyone tampering with her belief.

Before the Chinese herbal capsules ran out, Hope called Kathy, her gymnastics instructor, and began a cautious training program. It felt wonderful.

"Jeez, Hope," Kathy said, "you seem nearly as limber as before ... that awful day."

Hope shuddered, remembering "that awful day." During warm-ups of the biggest gymnastics event of the year a beginner doing back flips without watching where she was going had planted both her feet firmly in Hope's lower back. Hope recalled the crunching sound. But at the time, she chose to ignore it. Then, because of the injury, she landed wrong on her neck during her routine and trashed her cervical spine. Everyone said how lucky she was that she hadn't actually broken anything.

She didn't felt lucky when she had to give up gymnastics due to the searing pain and lack of mobility.

But now she had returned—out of pain and flexible as ever. However, she worried about running out of the medication. She *had* to get back to the Chinese Pharmacy. She'd been looking high and low for the business card for days, and, weirdly, couldn't find it. She felt nearly hysterical as she emptied the last capsule out of the dark brown, hand-blown glass bottle into the palm of her hand. Why didn't the label have the pharmacy's address on it?

It was night and Hope had no idea how late the pharmacy stayed open, much, *much* less how to find it. She had no clue how she'd stumbled on it in the first place. She threw on her coat and jumped in the car. Before long she'd wound her way among the strange little circuitous streets. And there was the pale green "Pharmacy" beckoning her in the next block. Greatly relieved, she parked the car then went through the jangling pharmacy door.

There sat the winsome pharmacist on his stool, looking just as if he'd been waiting for her.

"I'm so glad you're open! I'm so glad you're here! I'm so glad I found you—that is, I misplaced the business card, and ... and ...."

Hope noticed he was studying her carefully and she shut up while he checked her "body light."

"Well?" She asked after a few moments. "I just took the last capsule you gave me. I feel completely well. But what'll happen to me if I quit your medication all of a sudden?"

"Much better. Spine light happy all way up." He made tiny karate chop motions with the side of his hand to indicate her vertebra. "Down, light a little soft. Up, neck still weak, but both are much better." He began to gather the apothecary jars. "Need twenty more days herbal spine cure."

"I've started working on my gymnastics again. Do you think that's okay? My trainer says I'm almost as limber as before."

"Sure, sure. Exercise is very good. Your trainer takes good care of you. And you, are not to fall *crack!* on your back."

Hope looked at him sheepishly. "You're a very clever man, aren't you?"

"Um. Cleverness for young people like you. Mr. Chang is wise."

Hope nodded. "Hope agrees. Mr. Chang is wise."

"Hope? Pretty name. Nice name. But not just hope anymore, eh?"

"What do you mean?"

"Not just hope, *believe*." He put the little brown bottle in a sack and handed it to her.

Hope laughed. "That's true, Mr. Chang. How much do I owe you?"

"Seven dollars work well last time, yes?"

"Oh, absolutely, yes!" Hope handed him a ten, and, as he gave her change, a thought struck her. "Mr. Chang—I wonder if, well, you know, when

I hurt my back and stopped my gymnastics and my life changed so much, I also put on thirty pounds. And, even though I've started gymnastics again, I can't seem to lose any weight."

Mr. Chang began to bustle around behind the counter, putting the apothecary jars away and Hope thought she'd lost his attention altogether, but she stuttered on, "and, and, I wondered if, maybe, you have something, or know of something that would help me lose weight?"

There was a long silence and finally Hope peered over the counter. Mr. Chang was already putting a mixture in capsules. These he soon funneled into a pale amber bottle, affixed a label and wrote on it.

"Take one before meals. Metabolism go up, hunger go down, fat go out. You lose two-and-a-half pounds every week. In three months, thirty pounds gone."

"No!" Hope exclaimed.

"Yes," Mr. Chang said. "You must believe."

"I do! I will! How much?"

"Oh, five dollars. Easier to believe losing weight than repair back."

Three months later, Hope could hardly remember the year of her back injury, living incapacitated and inactive, like some chubby slug. Her back was well and her mirror reflected a svelte, trim gymnast. She was delighted, but with an edge of discontent.

Of course, Hope told herself as she studied her face in the magnifying mirror, there was a lot to be said for having one's spine healed and losing all of one's excess weight. But why stop there? She looked great, *for her age*, as everyone always said about other people. But why should she look thirty-three? Why not look twenty-one again? She just bet, no, she corrected, she believed Mr. Chang had something he could concoct that would make her look younger.

It was a Saturday morning and she'd *still* never found Mr. Chang's business card, but she got in her car and took off.

An hour-and-a-half later she hadn't found the strange little streets, but she managed to accidentally stumble on the movie theatre she'd been looking for when she first discovered Mr. Chang's Pharmacy.

"Maybe I don't really believe in something that will make me younger." Hope told herself taking a random left turn. And there she was, on Mr. Chang's street.

She drove up to the pharmacy, but there was no place to park. Hope hated to even circle the block for fear she'd lose the pharmacy again. She sat double parked and waited until someone pulled out. She made a mid-block U-turn and fairly flung her car into the parallel space, then ran across the street and through the jangling pharmacy door.

A squat, pale-skinned woman, with a head disconcertingly like Mr. Chang's, stood in front of the showcase, dusting. She turned and looked expectantly at Hope.

"Oh! Hi! I was, ahm, hoping to see, that is, is Mr. Chang here?"

The woman moved through beaded curtains behind the counter. Lilting exotic music of remote places came back to Hope from the inner sanctum behind the beaded curtain. Then Mr. Chang stepped through the beads. He studied her for a moment.

"Back is good. Every light even."

"Yes. And the thirty pounds!"

"Gone," Mr. Chang agreed. "Of course."

"I ... I wanted to thank you."

"No need to thank me. I know when people thankful without words and when people are not thankful with words."

"Well, I'm truly thankful, with and without words."

"And you are here now because ....?"

"Wise Mr. Chang! I'm here now because, oh boy, this is even more difficult than the weight thing."

Mr. Chang was getting down jars already. "Only one thing left," he said. "Youth."

Hope had a sudden insight into Mr. Chang's reality. Every day people came through his softly jangling door, wanting things in an inevitable sequence.

"Yes, Mr. Chang, youth." She moved close to the counter and watched Mr. Chang pour the blood red and bone white capsules into a crystal clear bottle.

"These you must take one every day," he said. "No more, no less."

Hope reached for the bottle before Mr. Chang even put it in a sack, but he ignored her as he methodically finished his preparations.

"How much do I owe you?" Hope asked.

"Getting younger hard to believe. Start out at fifteen dollars."

"Okay." Hope handed him the money. "Thank you, Mr. Chang, thank you."

Within days, Hope noticed that the fine lines around her eyes plumped up and smoothed out. Then the deeper ones. Her flesh came closer to the bone, and became nearly poreless again. Younger men found inane excuses to have a bit of conversation with her.

And she had a kind of energy she'd forgotten about, it had slipped away in such tiny increments. She was able to stay up almost all night and still be functional the next day.

She was young and thin and beautiful, and she felt pretty cocky about it.

When she was down to only two youth capsules, she drove straight to Mr. Chang's.

"Hi, Mr. Chang," she called cheerily as she came though the door. "See what you've done for me?" She pirouetted in front of the tall glass case and even considered for a fleeting moment doing a hand spring, but she had to hesitate because there was just barely enough room. Then she thought perhaps that was showing off too much.

"Hope is young," Mr. Chang observed.

"Hope," Hope agreed, "is young, and happy, and needs more youth capsules."

Mr. Chang was already busy with preparation. Hope watched him quietly for a few moments, but then, suddenly, a new insight came to her.

And, although a wee-little voice told her it was a dangerous question, it just came out.

"Mr. Chang ... I wonder why it is that you don't take this medicine yourself?"

"To make me young?"

"Yes."

Mr. Chang finished writing on the label and put the bottle in a sack then handed it to Hope. He looked at her with his deep, intelligent, wise, eyes and answered, "because I don't believe. That will be fifteen dollars."

Hope's mouth opened into a great, big, round 'O.' "You ... don't ... *believe?*"

"No."

Hope handed Mr. Chang the money, muttered "thank you," and shuffled out.

All the way home her mind kept repeating, "He doesn't believe!" How could *she* believe, if the creator of all her good fortune didn't believe? Especially with the way he preached belief.

Hope continued dutifully to take her "youth pills," but over the next few days, she was sure she saw small lines coming back into her face, and a couple weeks later she couldn't get into some of the new clothes she'd bought. The scale told her she'd gained ten pounds. A couple of days after that, Kathy pointed out that she was holding her neck. She hadn't noticed it consciously, but her neck had begun to throb.

Hope left the training session early and went home. She decided to go to a movie, which was how she usually coped with depression. She hadn't been to a movie in months.

Listlessly, she picked up the newspaper. The same theatre that had been having a Black & White revival when she first stumbled on Mr. Chang's pharmacy was having a Hitchcock marathon. She decided to go and let giant images of the common person getting abused wash over her, in complete miserable empathy, until she couldn't take any more.

She pulled on a jacket and drug herself out to her car.

But with an annoying sense of *deja vu*, Hope drove around unable to find the theatre, and finding herself, instead, once again, in front of the Chinese Pharmacy.

Resigned, she got out of the car and plodded to the door. She opened the door so quietly that it hardly made a sound. The odd thing was, as down as she felt, she was flooded with delight at the familiarity of the subtle scent of all the peculiar things combined.

"Hello, Hope," Mr. Chang said.

"Hello, Mr. Chang. Look at me!"

"I am looking."

"You gave me so much, then you took it away when you said you didn't believe."

Mr. Chang chatted as he gathered together a great many apothecary jars. "But I don't need to believe in the back medicine, because my back is not injured, or the weight-loss medicine because I always weigh perfect, or even youth medicine, which I do not desire."

He nodded as he mixed ingredients together. "I only need to believe in medicine that teaches me how to make medicine. What do I need with youth? Make me full of folly, and it would make me an inappropriate husband for my wife, who does not wish to be young again."

"Oh!" Hope exclaimed. "Why didn't you say that?"

"You didn't ask. Now you ask. People cannot hear an answer if they don't ask a question."

Hope felt a twinge of belief struggling around in her again. "Do you—do you have something that will help me believe, with my *own* belief?"

"Sure, sure." Mr. Chang put the one giant golden capsule he'd made into a small lavender bottle, and held it up to the light.

"How much?" Hope asked, reaching for it.

"One hundred dollars," Mr. Chang answered.

Hope's hand stopped in mid-air. "One hundred dollars?!"

"Sure, sure."

"May I ask, Mr. Chang, why this one capsule is so much more expensive than your other medications?"

"Because when you first came to me, you believed like a child. Then you get clever, you believe like someone who has to think about belief. This is the most difficult condition to cure. It must fix at once, or not at all."

Hope nodded. She scrounged through her purse and, including the don't-touch-but-for-dire-emergency hidden twenty dollars, she came up with one hundred dollars and two cents.

"You keep the two cents," Mr. Chang said, and laughed, *tee-hee.*

Hope laughed too. After all, she was getting her health, beauty, and youth back, and some wisdom too.

She suspected that the greatest of these was wisdom—if Mr. Chang's pricing had anything to do with it.

END

Angels to Nirvana

I was crawling around on the church floor after my Mardi Gras beads, which had mysteriously jumped their string and flown every which way in a wild jumble.

At that moment, in the middle of the rowdy carnival celebration on the street, a bunch of women came bursting through the door of the church. I took them for women's activists or Peace Corp workers. Don't ask me how I figured that, they just had an air of self-assurance and determination to change the world for better.

The first one came up to me as I squatted under a pew, gathering my beads. She stepped on one of them. It went *"crunch!"* under her shoe.

"What are you doing, sneaking around on the floor of the church?" she asked.

"I ..." I gestured at the beads, green and silver and orange all around her. "My string of beads broke, and I'm ...."

"Never mind." She waved to her peers, three other very sure-of-themselves women. They formed a half circle around her. Looking up at them, it was like a visitation. The street lights came through the stained glass windows making a halo around them, and it looked like the guardian angels had come right out of the stained glass windows to stand around me.

"This young man," she said, "has broken his string of Mardi Gras beads. Help him pick them up."

The three women fell to their knees and scrambled around for the beads, under the pews, in the aisles ... everywhere.

"How did you come to be in this church?" one of the women asked me. "Oh look, here's seven beads, all together."

"I don't know. I was in the street, celebrating ...." I looked into her eyes. They were that kind of hazel composed of green and brown and almost red segments. I stopped talking.

"Go on," she said.

I ... you ... your eyes ....."

"I know, kind of strange, aren't they?"

"But I've seen you ... Do you know me?"

She shrugged, but looked away.

"Do you know me?" I asked again.

"Here's another bead." She moved across the aisle on all fours, but somehow so gracefully, almost floating, as if performing a well-practiced dance move.

I scrambled after her. Clearly less graceful. "You know me, don't you?"

As she picked up another bead I reached out to stay her hand. A flash of light passed between our fingers.

"What the? ...." I sat back on my haunches, stunned.

The first woman came up to us, standing over us, disapproving.

"Just gather the beads!" she ordered.

The hazel-eyed woman moved away from me and picked up another bead. But she didn't hand it to me.

"Give me the bead," I said. She cautiously reached out her hand, her long fingers reaching toward me. She dared to look me in the eye. The flash of light passed between our hands again.

"*I know!*" I fairly shouted. Then quietly I said, "I know where I've seen you. In my dreams. In my dreams," I repeated. "Have you seen me? Do you know me?"

She looked behind me, over my shoulder.

"Yes," she whispered, "yes, I know you. But just leave me in your dreams. You don't want to bring me out into your real world."

"What do you mean? Here you are, in my real world."

A saxophone player belted out a song in the street, a song I've never heard but still, I could have hummed the tune.

Just gather the beads," she said. When you have 108, you'll arrive."

"What are you saying?"

"Count the beads—108—you'll arrive in nirvana."

I counted the beads, wanting only to look one more time into those strange, amazing eyes.

I counted 107 beads, then looked up, discovering that I sat on the sidewalk, under the saxophone player. He was about seven feet tall, his music came from far away.

"Hey ...." I asked him, "Hey, did you see a hazel-eyed woman? An amazing hazel-eyed woman?"

He looked down at me and again, I felt like one of the guardian angels in the church window had come alive. He didn't stop playing, but he nodded.

Yes, he'd seen her.

The faint lace of dawn crept up the sky behind the saxophone player, pink and pale orange. I looked down at my hands filled with Mardi Gras beads, longing to see the hazel-eyed angel again. But I knew I never would. For reasons clearly beyond my understanding, I was denied that one single bead to nirvana.

END

Spaceship House

When Aurora woke up, the bedroom was pitch black, which was strange because the street lamp in the alley always cast a shadowy light. She looked toward the clock radio, but there were no red glowing numbers. She reached for the headboard—her fingers walked along the shelf and found her watch. She picked it up, then pursued the little reading lamp and flipped its switch, but it didn't come on. The room was very, very cold.

Power out! Aurora concluded, strapping her watch on and thrashing about for her fuzzy slippers and fluffy robe. She still didn't understand the complete, the total darkness, and she still didn't understand what woke her up.

She felt her way along the wall of the hall and then she heard it, the deep, and way below deep, humming. A vibration so incredibly deep it was as much feeling as sound.

Aurora turned the corner of the hall into the dining room. Even though the entire north wall was windows and a door to the outside, it was black as black in here, too. She stumbled to the breakfront, opened a drawer and scrabbled around for the emergency candles and the lighter. After she lit a candle, she looked at her watch. 5:30. So early! She held the candle up to the anniversary clock on its shelf and it, too, read 5:30.

It's as if my house has become a spaceship in the night and transported me to a dark and vibrating place, Aurora thought. She shuffled to the dining room door and tried to open it, but the outer storm door wouldn't budge.

Trapped in my own house! She tried to tell herself she was being silly and melodramatic, but instead, an edge of sincere fear creeping up alongside her. She held the candle close to the glass. The door was like a mirror, she saw herself reflected in pale candle glow. Then she saw the faint grain of snow against the door. It had snowed to above the doors and windows in the night!

See now, Aurora, she reprimanded her fearful self, there's always a logical explanation for everything.

She hurried across the dining room and opened the sliding door to the living room. A pale light greeted her. The south side of the house had not drifted as high as the north. In the foyer she opened the front door. The snow was right up to the level of the front porch, as if there were no steps at all. It looked delightfully different to see the snow stretch out, all the trees shorter, and her gas yard lamp now only three feet tall.

Aurora walked out onto the porch—it was surprisingly warm, warmer than in the house. She watched the gigantic, wet snowflakes fall straight to the surface of the snow as if they were weighted. Before her eyes the snowflakes turned to rain.

"Weird." Aurora went back in the house and hurried to the bedroom. She lit the two fat candles on the dresser and threw on a couple of layers of clothing, then blew out the candles.

At the front door again, the world had become even more amazing. A foot of snow had already melted in the rain—she could see the top step to the porch. The heavily overcast sky strangely reflected candy-colored orange, pink, and lavender.

Aurora threw on a coat, scarf, mittens, boots, and grabbed an umbrella. Rain in Nebraska in January!

The sound and feeling of the peculiar thrumming vibration grew in intensity when she stepped out the door. The snow had sunk another couple inches, it had a plastic-coated sheen from melting so fast. Every branch and twig of every tree was loricated in ice.

Aurora crunched down into the snow. Here and there the ice held her up, but mostly she broke through. It was tough going. She wanted to get to the thrumming, although it seemed to come from everywhere, and she wanted to get to the source of the throbbing orange, pink, and lavender lights.

There was not another person to be seen. Aurora couldn't believe how happy she felt. She had no idea why she was happy, either. She hadn't been happy since Christmas day. On New Year's Eve Tom told her his New Year's resolution was that he was going to divorce her. Then he moved out the next day.

What was really strange, though, was, as broken-hearted and lonely and at odds with herself as she felt after Tom left, there were advantages. At first she'd really worried about how she'd live on her little pay check. But then she went grocery shopping and bought everything she loved, all kinds of vegetables, and beans—which Tom hated—and rice, and cheese, and bread.

She'd been stunned when her grocery bill was only thirty-five dollars instead of the usual hundred-and-twenty it was every week with Tom and his meat-eating. He ate pounds and pounds of pigs and cows and sheep.

Aurora struggled a couple of blocks through the snow and the odd, warm rain. There were power lines down everywhere, but she got around them without even really thinking about it. Every now and then there was a resounding CRACK! as a branch broke off a tree from the weight of ice, but it was muffled and muted by the vacuum of snow and close clouds.

And then too, she'd found herself thinking more and more lately about her acting career, the one she didn't have because Tom always told her she was a pie-in-the-sky dreamer, and she was no more an actress than his mom. Who was actually a pretty good actress, as Aurora had noticed, when she wanted something.

Aurora could see she was nearing the source of the candy-colored sky. She could no longer tell if the thrumming was a noise at all, it ran so completely in and out and up and down and through her.

The only thing that really annoys me, she thought, is how much I hate my job, although I've managed to save four-thousand dollars the last couple years fitting size sixteen women into size nine clothing.

But I'll never become an actress if I don't make a move.

She turned the corner and looked up. There was the source of the lights and the thrumming vibration. Aurora didn't know exactly what expectation she'd built up, but it had been something unearthly, something truly magical. Instead, a gigantic transformer, high on a power pole, was shorting out, or whatever it was doing, thrumming, and sparking the candy colors against the close clouds.

"It's still a wonderful sight and sound," Aurora said aloud, determined to keep her sense of wonder. Her own voice, which she could barely hear above the humming, sounded strange, like a chorus.

The vibration must be vibrating my voice box too, she reasoned. There was a logical explanation for everything. Aurora stood staring at the man-made transformer and felt the miracle of the morning fade. She turned to trudge back home.

"*Aurora!*" a chorus called to her.

She turned back, mouth open, and looked up to the lights in the sky. They dimmed and brightened as the chorus continued. "Aurora—quit your job, apply for an acting scholarship, go to school, you will become an actress who touches the hearts of many."

Right then a City of Lincoln Public Power truck came up and three men jumped out.

"Get back!" One of the men yelled to her.

"Watch out!" A second one called at the same time.

The third one just stared at her like she was crazy beyond description.

Aurora folded up her umbrella as it had stopped raining, turned, and headed for home, a happier-than-

Christmas feeling welling up in her, because she knew
now why she woke up so early.

There was a logical explanation for everything.

END

Sisters, Sisters

I've been a light rail driver since shortly before my conjoined twins were born on Christmas day, ten years ago. Talk about surprising someone with a present *not* done up in sparkly wrapping paper!

It's Christmas Day, and their tenth birthday ... the traffic is jammed up from the heart of town out to the rural reaches. As I fly by the stopped traffic, the motion making a stringed blur of all the bright red taillights, I think of my darling girls at home, cooking up their usual surprise.

On their sixth birthday, they decided to give me a birthday present. They already knew how much I loved the movie *White Christmas*, and they sang Sisters, Sisters ... which takes on a whole new meaning with the line, "Those who've seen us, know that not a thing could come between us."

We laughed until we cried. And then we cried. The girls' dad had visited the evening before, that Christmas Eve four years ago. I don't know why he came. He left us when the girls were a day old. Took one look at them and was out of there. Weird. It's his side of the family that has all the twins. There's never been one set of twins as far back as one can look in my family tree.

So ... I'm wondering what they'll surprise me with this year. It's been quite the year. In January all of the aliens—who've been here for years, as it turns out—made themselves publicly known. There are fourteen different kinds of humanoid aliens from all over the universe living on earth ... imagine!

Conjoined twins is not so unusual after this year.

All the predictions that people—that is to say, earthlings—would go into a panic meltdown if the aliens revealed themselves just ... did not happen. A lot of people had a lot of things to say about it for almost three weeks. Then the latest heart throb made a new movie, and that became the new big news.

I've finished my shift and one of my peers drops me off at the station two blocks from home.

"Have a nice Christmas with ... your girls," Marsha says as I get off the train.

"Thanks. I will. Merry Christmas to you, too." I wave. It starts to snow just as I approach home. Strange. It doesn't snow here anymore. Used to, but stopped with the earth shifting on it's axis. That happened three years ago. Also no big deal. Just ... climates changed.

I've always loved snow. Love it. I smile, even though I'm so mystified by this phenomena. Maybe the aliens are doing it. Some of them have that sort of ability.

I think, "Maybe it's the alien who's baby I saved."

A couple days ago, one of their funny looking little blue babies flew—yes, they fly—over the tracks, and somehow, the electrical matrix confused it. It just sat down on the rails. I happened to be walking up to my stop to ride to my shift at that moment. A train was coming Hell-bent-for-leather, and I knew the driver couldn't see the little blue baby on the tracks. I didn't think for a moment, I just ran out and grabbed that little thing ... he only weighed about three pounds, and I managed to save his—and my—life.

I come to my door and hear the lilt of "Sisters" from my girls. I step through the door and there's the alien mother with her blue baby flying around the living room.

Startled for a moment, I gather myself and try to say what I think I remember is "hi" in their language. But I'm stopped in mid-thought as I listen to my girls singing ... such lovely voices. But it sounds peculiarly stereo. Then, down the hall comes one of my girls ... *one of my girls!*

I can't understand what I'm seeing. From the door across the hall comes my other girl. "*Sisters, sisters*" they sing, as they come toward me, tears sparkling in their eyes.

"I disunited your children," the alien mother says in impeccable English. "Is that all right? Their organs were very taxed when united. Although I apologize if it's inappropriate for me to have done."

My girls fling their four lovely arms around me.

In shock, I can say nothing—then I finally gasp out, "Yes, it's ... it's *appropriate!*"

"*Sisters, sisters,*" we sing, crying with joy. Even the alien mother joins us, although she's clearly bemused by our display of emotion.

END

Across The Wolds

The late Autumn wind blew against the long, low, chalky hills of the Lincolnshire wolds. Twelve-year-old Cam Rafnal felt lonely to the bone. He recited, again, all the living creatures he'd seen, and taken the time to count, that day — five partridges, eleven lapwings, one brown hare, two pheasants, forty-four sparrows, and two-hundred-forty-nine sheep, looking like slow-rolling, shaggy boulders on the hills.

He was well-preoccupied with living things, given his occupation of undertaker's apprentice.

The sun sank fast, and Cam, his sandy hair standing every-which-way in the wind, encouraged his scruffy pony to hurry to their home over the horizon. Just as dusk pulled down the shade of darkness, a giant form, nearly as tall as the cart, loomed, then tumbled across the road in front of him.

The pony halted, his fuzzy little ears pointing back in fear. Cam couldn't find his breath for a minute, and when he did, it came fast and heavy. He and the pony peered into the murky dusk after the phantom.

"Must have been a weed. A huge, *huge* weed," Cam said to himself. "Get, ha!" He urged his intrepid pony, who hurried toward home willingly, soon pulling Cam and the rattly cart into the yard where several of Cam's siblings played.

At that very moment, his mother opened the back door to call the children in for supper. "There you are, Cam! I don't like you coming home this late, in the darkness."

"I don't like it either," he agreed, leading his pony to the shed.

The children ran into the house. Mother stood in the doorway, pulling her shawl close, watching Cam, then turned and closed the door behind her.

Cam unharnessed the pony, fed, watered, and brushed him perfunctorily. "I'll give you a good brushing tomorrow, Bonny Prince, but right now, I'm too hungry to stand." He closed the shed door and hurried into the house.

Inside, it was hot and full of life; eight children, parents, cats, a dog, a parakeet, all around cluttered with Victorian knickknacks, flashes of bright red and Prussian blue, velvet and moire, cushions and lamps, and *objets d' junque* piled upon themselves to the ceiling.

Nothing in perfect condition, nothing new, or even recent, but each and every pillow, lamp, picture, plate and foot stool contributed to the warmth and homeliness, every niche and cranny, filled with the fragrant ambiance of Mother's hot supper, exuded through chinks to the outdoors, and wafted on the chill air across the wolds.

"Cam, Cam, our Dad's home!" Kevin called as Cam through the door.

Dad stood by Mother, nibbling at the potatoes, telling her a story. A slow smile come into Mother's blue eyes until she burst out giggling.

Still upset, Cam wanted his dad to know it. He tried hard to feign no interest in Dad's story, even if everyone had quieted down to hear what made Mother giggle. After a few moments, the parents looked around at sixteen expectant, curious eyes.

"To the table, you band of ruffians!" Mother said, still laughing.

"Tell us the story, Dad," Kenward begged.

"Not for children," Dad waggled a stocky finger at them. "Now, to the table!"

"Aw, Dad!" the boys chorused, while all the girls, from Victoria to Katie, scurried to their places at the table.

"Well, then, boys, if you're going to stand around in the kitchen, help your Mother – here you go Kenward, take this salad, Cam, the potatoes, Colin, beans, Kevin, the bread, and I'll carry Mother."

Dad started to pick Mother up, the boys hooted and cheered, while Mother tweaked Dad's ear and protested. "You put me down, you!" Dad got her almost to the dining room before she struggled free.

"*Really!*" Victoria sat primly at her place, with a matronly air about her that belied her seventeen years.

"Queen Victoria disapproves," Kenward said, still laughing. "I just want to know, Ma, how you knew your first daughter would be so much like Her Royal Highness?"

"That's *enough*. Now sit, all of you boys, you too, Dad. Let's have a little civilization!"

"Or l-let's pretend we're in Wy-Wyoming territory, "Colin said, "L-like Uncle Jake."

This started a wild round of the boys doing their best vocal rendition of Indians and cowboys, while the girls put up an equally noisy protest about their noise.

Mother "shushed," and "hushed" and even Dad boomed "that's quite enough now," when a dull *thud*, then *thud-thud* sounded against the house. The entire family fell silent.

"What's that?" Katie finally whispered.

"It's a ghost," Cam whispered back.

"Nonsense, Cam," Dad said, "We won't have any such talk around here." He stood, threw on a coat and went out the back door, Kenward following.

Cam looked around the table at the paled complexions of his dark-haired sisters, each an approximate replica of their beautiful mother, and at his two ginger-haired, usually ruddy-faced brothers, who, together with himself and Kenward were peas from the same pod as their ginger, stocky dad.

The wind increased, whining and sighing, around the house.

"There's Dad," Kevin whispered.

They could just barely hear the rumble of Dad's voice through the wall, then Kenward's higher rumble answered. Then an ugly *"scra-a-a-p-ing,"* noise against the house.

"Ah-ooh!" Everyone said, looking at each other, then bursting into nervous giggles.

Dad and Kenward came through the back door, chuckling like drinking buddies.

"Well?" Mother and Victoria asked in unison.

"It was a huge weed," Dad said. "Huge. Practically as big as me. Come on, let's eat!"

"I know that weed," Cam said. "It tried to scare me on the way home."

"You must be leading a lonely life, haunted by a dead weed!" Kenward reached across and tousled Cam's wild hair.

Even Dad guffawed as he heaped food onto his plate. "Come on now, eat, Cam, my boy. You've had a long, hard day, dealing with the deceased in both animal and plant kingdoms."

Although weak with hunger, a righteous anger rose in Cam. He sat, flushed and silent.

"Cam," Mother said after a few minutes, "aren't you feeling well?"

"I hate it!" he shouted. "I hate it, and you ... laugh at me." The force of his anger kept him from imagining more words.

"Lower your tone," Dad said.

"I though you got over that," Mother said quietly.

Cam shook his head.

"But you haven't said anything in so long."

"I didn't get over it."

"You had to have a pony," Dad said. "With ten human mouths to feed around here, we can't have livestock that doesn't pay for itself one way or another. Now all you boys futures are accounted for – Kenward apprenticed to a farm, you to the undertaker, Colin I'll train with me, and we'll be able to sent Kevin to medical school by the time he's ready."

"But Dad, I want to be with *you*. How can you have Colin? He st-stutters! I think it's the funniest thing I ever heard, an auctioneer who stutters. Ha!"

All of Cam's brothers and sisters stared at Cam with their eyes wide round. No one ever questioned Dad, and no one ever, *ever* made fun of Colin's stutter.

"For that very reason," said Dad quietly, "for that *very* reason am I apprenticing Colin to myself. Shame on you for making fun of his affliction."

Cam looked down at his plate of food, aghast with himself. At least he'd gotten one question answered. Until now, he couldn't understand how his Dad could prefer Colin as his apprentice. But it still didn't answer why *he'd* been apprenticed to an undertaker – as punishment for falling in love with Bonny Prince? But all his sisters had begged for the pony as much as he.

"I know you're angry, Cam, but one day, when you're living in the finest house of any of us, you'll thank me. There'll always be a living to be made by undertakers. And even, although more modest no doubt, auctioneers. Now, eat, eat, eat!"

*　*

That night Cam lay awake thinking about his future until long after the heat in the house cooled to a midnight chill, until even long after the slick porcelain shard of white moon skated by his little window.

He'd never thought about the far-away, grown-up future. He'd thought about tomorrow, or next season, or even as far as next year. Last month, as soon as they'd returned from the Goose Fair in Nottingham, he thought about going again next year.

But now, he found himself puzzling over that long distant time his Dad seemed readily able to plan and imagine on his behalf. He tried to see himself in the position of his employer, Mr. Horton. To see himself long and skinny and somber, and doing the work Mr. Horton did. But that future receded into an opaque nothingness. He saw no grand house, no well-placed acquaintances, and certainly no laboring over corpses.

But a small flame flickered remotely down the tunnel to the future. Cam tried to reach its promised warmth, but exhaustion claimed him and he slipped from the tunnel to the future, into the quiet pond of his dreams.

The next afternoon, Mr. Horton summoned Cam into the luxurious, dark cavern of his office. "Young man, I need you to retrieve Mr. Knox, I believe the Knox residence is near your home?"

"Yes sir, next to us but one, that's right. Mr. Knox has business with you?"

Mr. Horton allowed the muscles in the lower third of his face to pull horizontally. Cam had only seen this happen once or twice before and he'd come to the conclusion it had to be what passed for a smile in Mr. Horton's imagination. "You could say he has business with me, yes. Mr. Knox passed away last night."

"But ... I saw him just last week, talking with my Dad. He was perfect."

"Nevertheless, his heart gave out on him last night, which fact employs both you and me today. Please be at it, as it's already late in the day."

"Yes sir." Cam hurried out to his cart.

All during the horrible ride to the Knox farm, the oppression of his apprenticeship weighed more and more heavily. It felt nearly unendurable to pass his home—dreadful, black imaginings of being sent some day to collect someone from behind the safe portals of his beloved honey-colored, limestone home made him cry, the bitter wind stung his eyes and turned the warm tears to freezing cold against his cheeks.

When he pulled into the Knox courtyard, Mr. Knox's brother helped Cam carry in the thin wooden coffin Mr. Horton provided for transport. Inside, the house was dark as night, with Mr. Knox stretched out on the dining room table, looking very much as though he'd chosen to take a nap there. A rosy cast remained about his features, and Cam could not convince himself Mr. Knox no longer resided among the quick.

Mrs. Knox, in black from head to foot, her face covered with a veil, sat immovable by her husband. For a large sum Cam would have been willing to wager she was the deceased. Mr. Knox's pale, fragile, little boy sat by his mother, all in black as well, a study of confusion and curiosity on his child's face, staring at his father.

There were two other adult males standing about. When Mr. Knox, the living, and Cam put down the coffin, an elderly woman removed Mrs. Knox and her son from the room.

Muddled, Cam helped awkwardly – he knew these people, but they behaved as if unaware of his presence. It seemed like a dream, and the people in the dream didn't know he dreamt them.

Before long, the coffin, with Mr. Knox cozily inside, was loaded onto Cam's cart. The surviving Mr. Knox gently placed a blanket around his brother, then placed the thin lid over him.

Cam nodded, climbed onto the cart, pulled out onto the road and headed for the undertaker's. He thought with dismay how tonight he'd be even later than last night arriving home. Cam left off concentrating on the rutted road, and the cart slipped with a *"thunk!"* into the ruts, and the lid slipped off the coffin.

"Hic!" Mr. Knox said.

Cam reigned the pony to escape the ruts, the cart "bump-bumped" out of the ruts.

"Hiccough!" Mr. Knox insisted without equivocation.

Cam pulled the pony to a stop, stood and looked back at Mr. Knox. He got down from the cart and walked back to his passenger. "Mr. Knox?"

Mr. Knox said nothing.

"You ... you can talk to me, Mr. Knox. I'm not afraid. I can't believe you're dead anyway, so if you're not, that's fine. Mr. Horton pays me the same either way."

Still, the reposeful Mr. Knox declined to make further comment.

Cam looked up at his home in the near distance. In the advancing dusk, lights burned in Victoria's window and the kitchen window. Dad would still be home, getting ready for his circuit through Louth tomorrow. It could do no harm to stop and have him take a look at Mr. Knox.

"Mr. Knox, if you're there, I'll have my Dad try to talk to you, if you don't mind."

He hurried Bonny Prince up the road and into the shed, then jumped down and ran into the house. Mother stood at the stove.

"Is my Dad home?"

"You're early tonight!" Mother smiled on him. "He's out chopping wood."

Cam ran back out and around the house where Colin and Dad were hacking logs into fireplace size.

"Dad! Come see Mr. Knox."

"Is he here?"

"Yes. That is, Mr. Horton had me get him. They thought he died, but he hiccoughed! Twice! And I ... I don't think he's dead, Dad."

"My God ... goodness ... where is he?"

"In the shed." Cam turned and ran to the shed, his dad following. He came into the shed and looked at Mr. Knox. He felt Mr. Knox's neck and then his wrist for a pulse. He stepped back from the cart.

"He's dead, Cam."

"Are you sure?"

"He's cold, he has no pulse, and ... well, he's dead. Can't you tell?"

"I can't. Ever since I saw him on the dining room table, he seemed alive."

"He's not. How did he die?"

"Mr. Horton said his heart quit last night. But Dad, he's younger than you ...."

"It happens, Cam. Entirely possible. Well, you'd better get him to Mr. Horton's." Dad looked out the shed door at the complete darkness and cold sky. "No, it's too late. You might as well unharness the pony. It looks like Mr. Knox will have the pleasure of the hospitality of our pony's shed this night."

"Dad! You can't leave Mr. Knox out here!"

"What would you have me do with him?"

"Carry him in the house."

"No. Oh, no! I won't have a corpse under my roof over night."

"But Dad, it's too cold out here."

"He won't mind." Dad turned and walked out of the shed.

Slowly Cam unharnessed Bonny Prince and attended to his other chores. Before he went into the house, he tucked Mr. Knox's blanket in around him. "Sorry about Dad, Mr. Knox, but I'm sure you know he's set in his ways ... I'll leave the lid off, so you can watch the moonlight if you want."

The mood at dinner was subdued as the idea of Mr. Knox in the shed sobered everyone. Dad insisted they all go to bed early, since he himself had to get up before dawn. Soon the house became still with only the rhythm of breathing.

But Cam could not sleep. His eyes focused on the ceiling, his mind on Mr. Knox. Unthinkable that the poor man must stay out in the freezing night! The unthinkable became unbearable, and Cam pulled the fat woolen blanket from his bed, stole downstairs and put on boots, coat, gloves, and hat and went out to the shed. The feeble moon slipped behind clouds as he opened the shed door providing the merest shadow of light in which to see the cart. He flung his blanket over Mr. Knox.

"I feel sorry about you being out here all night, when it's so cold. But it doesn't do to oppose my Dad." Cam turned a bucket over and sat on it by the cart. "Take my case—I hate being apprenticed to the undertaker. But Dad has something in mind, so that's the end of it."

"*Haum-hmmm.*" Mr. Knox cleared his throat and sat up.

Cam leapt to his feet, taking a step back. He wished he could see better, but what he did see was Mr. Knox sitting, stiffly, his hands still crossed over his chest.

"Don't take it so, lad, that your Dad has me stay out here for the night. It doesn't bother me in the least."

"You're sure?" Cam asked in a squeaky, breathless voice.

"Quite. However, I wanted to thank you for your concern. You're a good boy at heart."

"Thank you, sir. I just ... I worried about you."

"Well, you needn't. I have no use for hearth or blanket."

"You're *sure?*"

"I'm sure."

"Then, Mr. Knox, may I ask you a question?"

"Certainly."

"Are you dead?"

"Oh, yes, Cam. I'm well and truly dead. That is to say, this body is dead. The real me, however, is most pleasantly free."

"Really?" Cam knew he would spend a lot of time pondering the idea of not having one's body as a condition of freedom. "You sound happy to be free."

"Most sincerely."

"Can you tell me about it?"

"Well, I wouldn't want to spoil your afterlife for you. But I do have something to tell you about your life—which is this—you want to follow in your Dad's footsteps and be a traveling auctioneer. This is because you have two great loves which you haven't understood yet. One is, you have a great love of traveling, your soul longs to see every place and everything and every sort of person. The second is, your Dad's profession has given you a love of the sound and poetry and magic and power of words. I'll tell you something more, if you promise not to tell your father I told you."

"I promise," Cam agreed.

"You'll not become an undertaker. In fact, your time as an apprentice is quite limited. You're going to be a writer—precisely speaking, a journalist. You'll travel to amazing places and be a part of history in the making." Mr. Knox relaxed in the pale light.

"Not only you, but your son as well. Only he's going to write novels." Little by little he reclined back into his narrow bed. "Of course, you'll have to apply yourself to your studies, they won't have machines to check your spelling for quite some time."

"What?"

"Apply yourself to your studies."

"Of course."

"You may take your blanket back. I have no use of it, and you, a sturdy boy with blood throbbing through you body like an excellent machine, need it."

Cam reached out and carefully removed his woolen blanket. "If you're sure."

"I am. Thank you so much, Cam Rafnal, for your kindness."

"You're welcome, sir."

A cold stillness permeated the shed that convinced Cam only he and his pony were here—with no more presence to Mr. Knox than the wood surrounding him.

"Good night, Mr. Knox. Good night, Bonny Prince," Cam said, closing the shed door, then hurrying back to his safe, warm bed.

* *

And so Cam was not surprised the next day when Mr. Horton called him into his dark den and told him one did not keep a corpse overnight, and also, because of his relentlessly cheerful disposition, he felt Cam ill-suited for an undertaker's apprentice.

When Dad returned a few days later, Cam went outside to tell him of Mr. Horton's decision before anyone else could. Dad didn't look at Cam while he unloaded the wagon. "And what's to become of you, boy? If you can't see your way though anything, what's to become of you?"

"Don't worry, Dad. I know what's to become of me – I'm going to travel the world, I'm going to be a journalist."

Dad stopped his work and gave Cam a disappointed look. "Wherever do you get such a bizarre idea, and how will it come to pass when you can't even apply yourself to your school work?"

"I'm going to do better than ever in school. I have to prepare for the future."

Cam watched as his dad scrutinized his face, and he seemed to see something he'd not noticed before. "Well ... perhaps you're right. I can't see as a journalist has any security, but I guess you're too full of life to work with the dead."

Cam nodded, "That's right, Dad. Well, anyway I learned something working for Mr. Horton. I learned that even the dead can teach you about life."

END

Blythe Ayne – 83

Pagoda Dragon

Raul entered through the beaten up alley door of the Pagoda Dragon, *slap, slap!* only to face an appalling mountain of dishes. The last of the waitresses flung off her apron, looking harried and sore-footed, squinting at Raul like somehow her sore feet were his fault, then left without so much as a good-night.

"*Ack!* She's ugly anyway, man," Raul said to himself.

The busboy brought in one last, gigantic stack of dishes. " 'Night," he muttered as he slunk through the alley door, *slap, slap!* leaving the kitchen and its mammoth pile of labor to Raul. Raul hated washing dishes—as if anyone could like it—but he knew he hated it more than like a bazillionaire if he had to do dishes, or more than like the world's most beautiful model if she had to do dishes.

He spent his whole entire day hating the thought of washing dishes, then he spent the whole entire night hating the doing of washing dishes. He was full of a hate focused on one event.

Raul decided he'd practice his karate first, the sight of dishes piled so high that they practically blocked out the light was beyond repulsive—he just couldn't, couldn't, *couldn't* bring himself to start on them. They'd be the end of him, he thought. His life would go down the drain, washing dishes.

He spied the mop handle, bereft of its raggedy head which must be in the laundry, behind the door to the dining room. An excellent weapon! Raul had only had half-a-dozen karate lessons, and was far from knowing how to wield a weapon, in fact, his own hands were a danger to him. In the last class he'd hit himself in the face and still sported a bloody scab on his nose—which he'd used as an excuse to call in sick.

But he made up for his lack of training by his intensity of hate. He grabbed the mop handle, picturing himself lean and graceful and svelte.

"*Yi, yi, yi,*" he yelled. He crashed through the double swinging doors to the dining room, leaped onto the seat of a booth, to a table, thrashing the mop handle through the air, cracking one of the hanging lanterns, setting it into a crazy motion, casting berserk patterns of shadow and light around the room. The walls and ceiling, covered in gilt and red carved dragons leapt alive.

Raul became incited to even more frenzied action, leaping from table to table, prodding the delicate Chinese lanterns into motion, dragons moving about in their shadowed spaces like caged and angered creatures, so many enemies to be conquered.

"*Yeah!* Take that," Raul shouted, teasing one small wooden dragon with the end of his death-appointing mop handle. He attempted to twirl the stick in his hands. It appeared such an easy thing when he watched martial arts movies, but quite a different matter in practice, and he felt the stick come, *whack!* in brutal contact with something above. He looked up just in time for a chunk of the tail of the sixteen-foot carved dragon on the ceiling to plop on his forehead and to the floor.

"Oops." Raul climbed down and picked up the gild wooden scales, turning it over in his hand. He almost felt badly for a moment, but the anger welled up in him again. "*Yeah, yeah,*" he hollered at the dragon. "Serves you right, all of you, make me do this hateful job. I don't feel bad at all. No. *I feel good!*" Raul threw down the dragon's scales and picked the mop handle up again. "Yeah, it feels good!" He reached up and poked at the golden, serpentine dragon, now intent on breaking its scales, consumed by anger and indignation.

How strangely the shadows move although the lanterns have finally stilled, how undulating the dragon, how lazily its scales ripple, how livid the slow burn of fury in its eye. Raul backed into a booth, trying to understand what he saw, but there wasn't time for him to give the phenomena much consideration.

* *

"That lazy little toad," Mr. Fung said the next morning when he went into the kitchen and saw the dishes untouched. He sighed deeply, rolled up his sleeves and started to work, making a mental note to put an ad in today's paper for a dish washer.

During lunch a customer looked up from her lover's eyes to the beautiful gilt dragon carved in the ceiling above and was about to comment on its beauty, but said instead, "look, George, what's coming out of that dragon's mouth?"

George, intent on eating quickly and getting some "recreation" in before the noon hour was over, glanced up and shrugged. "Looks kind of like a hand holding a broken stick."

"*Eugh,* it does! Hmm ... I thought Chinese dragons were benign." Martha returned her attention to her meal and George.

END

Time, Time, Time

*D*r. *Justin Williams*, Psychiatrist is printed in tall, square-cut letters on the smoky glass door. Beneath that, in smaller letters, it adds: *Psychiatrist*

I've never been to a psychiatrist. I wonder how he might be able to help me. Will he have the same prejudices I've been encountering since arriving here when people take in my long, tangled hair, my rumpled clothes? I've heard them say "hippie" behind my back.

But I'm not a hippie. I mean, I'm pretty sure I'm not. The truth is, I don't know what a hippie is.

I enter the doctor's office. A pretty girl sits behind an imposing receptionist's desk, engrossed in her work. I sidle up to her.

"What're you doing?" I ask quietly.

She jumps. Her petite frame actually leaves the chair. "Oh! You startled me." She pulls away from me, taking me in from head to foot—my disheveled hair, my torn dove gray dress, dirty hem dragging on the floor, my scuffed high top button shoes.

"I'm sorry," I apologize. "What are you doing?"

"I'm correcting the doctor's spelling. He can't spell to save himself."

I feel dubious about putting my life in the hands of a doctor who can't properly spell.

"What can I do for you?" she asks, pulling a bit farther away from me.

"I'm Elvira Green. I have an appointment."

She looks at her appointment book, a huge, complicated affair. "You're early."

"Am I?"

"You're appointment's not until three. It's eleven-fifty."

"Is it?"

"Don't you have a watch?"

"Yes." I hold out my wrist to show her my delicate solid gold watch.

"It's beautiful!" She looks at me as if a camel just came through the door wearing a tutu.

"Yes."

"Let me see it." I hold my wrist closer to her. "It says six o'clock."

"Yes."

"It doesn't work." She shrugs. "The doctor is out to lunch. He has two patients after lunch, then you."

"All right," I move across the waiting room and sit on a luxurious sofa.

"What are you doing?"

She seems a bit slow. "I'm ... waiting," I answer as if talking to a small child.

"Until *three!?*"

"Yes."

"You can't wait here."

"Why not?"

"Because…because…." She can't actually formulate a reason.

I look off into middle distance, knowing she'll tell me when my appointment is as soon as she can.

Sure enough, a couple of minutes later she's saying, in a stiff, unpleasant tone, "The doctor will see you now."

"Thank you." I follow her into a large office. A beautiful grandfather clock chimes three.

"Hello Miss Greene," the doctor says. "Wendy tells me you've been in the waiting area since before noon."

"Yes. She told me that, too." I look around his plush office, startled by articles pinned to the wall as if they're some kind of decoration. "May I ask where you got this parasol?"

"My wife found it at some antique shop. I let her decorate my office. She loves that sort of thing."

"I see."

"Please be seated and tell me what's on your mind today."

I relax into a big wing-backed chair. "I don't know what you can do to fix my problem, but the other day an elderly woman approached me on the street and said you had helped her niece when she was lost."

"And what is *your* problem?"

"I don't know what a hippie is."

"Oh, well, that's not really a problem."

"But I keep hearing people call me that. I thought I ought to know what people here think of me."

"Hummmmm," he says, very drawn out. "What do *YOU* think of what they're calling you?"

"I don't know. I'm asking you."

"Tell me more."

"As I say, I'm lost."

"We all feel lost at times...."

"No, I mean, I'm truly lost. I woke up one day, and found myself here. Everything is so, so strange. I want to go home."

"Where's home?" He seems nearly as simple-minded as the girl at the big desk.

I talk slowly. "Again ... I'm lost. If I knew where home is, I'd be there."

He nods. "What's it like where you come from?"

"Where I come from, my watch is correct. The parasol on the wall, and these other things you have hanging around, are in my home. They're not ... antiques."

"Are you saying you're from a different time?"

"Yes."

He starts to write fast and furiously on a big yellow tablet.

"Are we through?" I ask, seeing him thus engaged.

"No ... no. Continue. You think you're from a different time." He keeps writing.

"I don't think it, I know it ...."

"Tell me more," he says.

"The other day, I went to sleep on a nice woman's sofa, and woke up *IN THE STREET!*"

He pauses in his writing and gives me a studied look. "What medications or substances have you taken?"

"Nothing! I'm telling you, I'm leaping around through time ...." I begin to feel angry. I know I must control intense emotion—it drives these inexplicable time leaps. But he's supposed to know about this, isn't he? Didn't the sweet lady tell me he'd know how to fix my problem? Hadn't she pulled out that amazing device from her handbag that connected her to this office?

Frustration wells up into rage. I want to shout ... which I've never done in my life.

But just as I open my mouth, I pop out of his office. I'm by a rushing river where half a dozen unimaginably gigantic animals stand drinking.

Terrified, I also feel a thrill of satisfaction. "See?" I say to the doctor, who will not make an appearance on time's stage for eons.

One of the gargantuan creatures spies me. I slink into the underbrush, my high top shoes sinking into the fecund earth. Giant, humid leaves stick to my dress as I move into the shadows.

I gather my skirts around me, close, to make myself small. I glance at my watch. Five till eight. Somewhere in the faint, undreamed of mists of time, my family is either finishing breakfast, or is sitting before a cozy evening fire, wondering where I am. Or, if I'm *here*, before the dawn of time, do I exist *there* at all?

I sit. I wait. Here before the dawn of time, I pray for another leap that will take me home.

END

Ix-Chel and the Iguana

"**I**f you were going to Europe, I'd consider it," Todd said.

"It's not a multiple choice question." Mimsey folded up the brochure full of pictures of blue water, blue sky. "Your father and I have decided to go to Cozumel and you're coming with us."

"If I don't go you'll save a pile of money, and get to be alone with each other." Todd felt a twinge when he saw the disappointment shadow his mother's face—but it was just a twinge.

"Look, Todd…" Mom's voice was soft and low, "you're going to college in two months and then—your childhood's over. You don't care what this means to me, do you?"

"It doesn't have anything to do with all that stuff about the passing of childhood. I just don't want to be bored into a zombie mucking around in Mexico."

"But it's a beautiful island, see?" She shoved the brochure into his face. He took it from her. "It's lovely, isn't it? And you'll get a great tan. You'll get golden brown in a week, and ... you and your father can spend some quality time together. He won't have anywhere to run off to."

"Well, whoopie," Todd said sarcastically. "The time for that is kind of passed, Mom. Why do you want to go there, anyway?"

"Because the accommodations are excellent, and the beaches are beautiful. The travel agent went there last summer and she said it's wonderful. They have these little kitchenettes and ...."

Todd shoved a picture from the brochure at Mimsey and she shrank back. "How about these things, Mom—your favorite!"

She snatched the brochure out of his hand and turned the page. "It's just an iguana. The literature says they're not dangerous."

"I can't believe you'd go *any*where that reptiles are running around loose." Todd got satisfaction in seeing his mother give a little shudder, then collect herself.

"There can't be all that many. Anyway, what's interesting about Cozumel is that the ancient Mayan women considered it sacred. They'd boat over from the mainland and have fertility rituals. Archaeologists still find dolls the women gave to the fertility goddess as offerings."

"Oh boy!" Todd said. "From one matriarchy to another."

"What matriarchy? I have your father's last name, and no authority. I can't even get you to go on a family vacation without a major argument."

Todd picked up the brochure again and glanced at the pictures. He now noticed a pretty serious ratio of babes to sea, sand, and sky. "Okay, I'll go." He got up and ambled from the dining room. He didn't even bother to watch the relief and pleasure flood his mother's eyes. She was too easy. And when things were too easy, you didn't get to have a really satisfying emotion. He wished that, just once, he could feel whatever it was his mother felt about the small things. Like now, the—whatever she felt—just because he said he'd go with them on their stupid vacation.

He had to laugh at Mom's notion that he and Dad would have some great breakthrough. Or even a conversation! Dad hadn't had anything to say to him over the last seventeen summers, why would this summer be any different?

*   *

"Okay, do we have everything?" Mimsey fluttered around the carry-on luggage like a hen around chicks.

"Mom, relax, we're at the airport. If we don't have everything, we're not about to go home and get it now, are we?" Todd was stretched out, his feet nearly across the aisle so that his mother had to step over his legs as she clucked around.

"You're right, Todd dear, of course. I count five pieces of carry-on luggage. I'm sure I counted six before we left home. I distinctly remember saying to myself 'six.'"

"Well, Dad, guess you'll have to run home and get whatever's missing."

"What's that?" Brad was sitting two seats over from Todd, his face buried in the financial section of the newspaper. In no way would a passing stranger have thought he had any relationship to the tall, thin, dark-haired, blue-eyed son and mother, who themselves had features that mirrored one another.

Blythe Ayne – 97

"Of course he's not going home. Whatever we left behind will just have to stay behind. It's just that I was so sure I said 'six' before we left."

"You said 'five,' Mom. I was there and I heard you say 'five carry-on and four check-in'. Dad was there too, but of course he didn't hear you say anything. As usual."

"What's that?" Brad mumbled from behind the paper.

"Don't bother your father," Mimsey said.

"Heaven forbid." Todd mimicked Mom's voice. "Heaven forbid that our vacation would start now, and Dad would begin talking to us, like you said he would."

"You're sure I said 'five'?"

"Absolutely positive."

"Why would I think I said six? That's strange ...."

"Flight number forty-seven to Cozumel, now boarding. Those passengers with boarding passes for rows ...."

"That's us!" Mimsey grabbed luggage.

"What's that?" Brad asked.

"We're boarding, Brad. Come on!"

Todd and Mimsey stood and waited while Brad meticulously folded his paper and stuck it under his arm, then finally stood. At last he reached for the one remaining bag.

"Let's go!" Mimsey scurried through the door and down the hall to the plane.

*   *

Todd couldn't have been more relieved when the plane landed. Between Mom's nervous energy and Dad's comatose newspaper-hiding, he'd had twice more than enough of the both of them. All he could think about was getting into his own room.

The good news was, a couple hours into the flight, Mom had finally quit going on about that sixth piece of carry-on luggage. Which started up again when they deplaned.

"Okay, Todd, do we have everything?" Mom asked, gathering luggage. "Let me count. Five pieces—what's missing?"

"Oh, *migod!*" Todd was ready to snatch something off the shoulder of an innocent co-traveler and offer it to his mother. "There are *five*, Mom. Five. One-two. Three-four. Five. That's it. That's all there was, that's all there is. Jeez, *pul-ease!* Leave me some remnant of sanity."

Mimsey looked at Todd with her mouth hanging open. "My goodness, Dear Heart, you don't have to make such a production. It just slipped my mind. I remember. It's five."

Todd shook his head in disgust. "Thirty-seven years old, and senility already setting in."

"Todd," Brad said, "show your mother some respect."

"It speaks!" Todd observed.

The three of them came up to customs, both of his parents glaring at him as they fell into line. Todd felt pretty smug—it wasn't often he was able to push both their buttons in practically the same breath.

After customs, they took a taxi, then a ferry to Cozumel. Todd was tempted to ask, "what next, donkey cart?" But didn't have the energy to try and start up anything. All he could think about was getting into his own room. At least there would be a wall between him and the crazies. And the sooner he got next to some girl, the better. But for now he just wanted to shower and crash out.

"Okay, sweetie," Mimsey said after they checked into the hotel and got to their rooms, "throw your things down, grab a quick shower and let's go have dinner."

"No way, Mom. I'm wiped out."

"We're all tired, dear. We'll have just a little something to eat and make an early night of it." Mimsey closed their room door behind her. Brad had already slunk absent-mindedly through the doorway.

"Oh for!...." Todd turned, unlocked his door, stepped into the room and slammed the door, "God's sake!"

Somehow he got through dinner. But how, he wondered, could he get through this week? And in addition to everything else, he hadn't seen even one potential babe since he got here. Not one! Old couples and families with little kids. The only decent looking woman was apparently on her honeymoon with a Mr. Universe look-alike.

Todd woke up early the next morning to reconnoiter the territory. It wasn't so bad once the old folks, including his own, were out of view.

He meandered to the pool. There was that honeymoon-er—the woman—swimming laps in an otherwise un-populated pool. Going around like nobody's business, and Mr. Universe nowhere in sight. They must both be athletes. Todd spent a couple minutes fantasizing about how the two of them had met at the Olympics.

Soon he found his mind wandering to the sorts of things they maybe did with each other. It was a short trip to re-place Mr. Universe with himself. And, watching her firm, muscular body in a sea green one-piece suit cut through the water with a fierce rhythm, it was an exceptionally pleasant pastime—until she looked up and lost her rhythm with the intensity of his stare.

Chagrined, Todd turned and went back into the hotel restaurant to order breakfast, charging it to his room. The satisfaction he got out of being able to tell Mom he'd already had breakfast when she started nagging him to join them helped take the edge off the embarrassment he still felt at being caught staring at that woman like a little kid.

Then "Mr. Universe" came into the restaurant. Life was cruel. He could picture the wife coming in shortly, pointing Todd out to her husband, leaning over and whispering something to him and both of them giggling. The thought ruined his breakfast, which hadn't even arrived yet.

When it came, he wolfed it down and hurried out.

On the way back to his room he saw a sign advertising skin-diving lessons, right there at the hotel. More pictures with young, beautiful women. Even without the women, the idea sounded pretty good. Have some adventure, and get away from Mom as a bonus. Maybe he'd take lessons every afternoon.

"Oh! There you are!" Mom called from down the hall. "I was just knocking on your door. Come along with us to breakfast."

"I had breakfast."

"Without us? Why would you do that?"

"Because I woke up early and I was hungry, that's why."

"Well, you can just spend a few minutes with your father and me. It's not as if you have anything else to do."

Without a word, Todd turned and walked with his parents back to the restaurant. He knew the young wife would be there by now. Sure enough, there they both were.

When the waiter led them past her table, she looked up and smiled—no, smirked, Todd was sure. At least her husband ignored him.

After that humiliation, the negatives just piled up. They were seated only one table away from the honeymooning couple, and, after his parents ordered their breakfast and Dad made himself invisible behind the financial section, Mom started in.

"Guess what, dear?"

"What?" Todd morosely studied the monogram on his napkin.

"I was looking at the booklet in the room about the hotel? Did you look at it?"

"No."

"Well, they have this skin-diving class every afternoon. I'm going to go to it. I thought you might like to go, too. Wouldn't that be fun?"

"You're going skin-diving?"

"Sure. Why not?"

Todd shrugged. "No reason not."

"So, are you with me? You know your father won't do it, he's such an old poop!"

"What's that?"

"I don't think so, Mom," Todd answered. "We did scuba diving last year when our sneak group went to San Diego."

"So you won't keep your old mom company?"

"I'm keeping you company now. We're not Siamese twins!"

"Of course we aren't. Don't say such a thing."

Todd wished he knew what it was that every time he said something like that, Mom got visibly uncomfortable. Even if he didn't understand it, he got satisfaction out of doing it.

Mimsey quietly finished her breakfast. "Well, maybe I won't do it then."

"Not do what?"

"The skin-diving thing."

Todd shrugged. "I'm going back to my room." Whywhywhy was there this endless contest of wills between them?

That evening at dinner, Mimsey jabbered on and on about the skin-diving class, which she'd decided to go to after all. Brad and Todd ate in silence.

"But I guess I might miss the class tomorrow."

Todd tore his attention from the view of sand and water. "Why?"

"Because we have to tour the Mayan ruins."

"Why do we have to?"

"Because they're here. Doesn't it sound like fun? Adventure! Exploring!"

"It sounds hot and boring."

"Well, it won't be. Your father's coming too, and we're going to have a great time if it kills us."

"Great," Todd muttered. Now he'd have to spend the rest of the evening trying to figure out some excuse not to go on a stupid tour of a pile of rocks.

* *

Well, here I am, among piles of stupid rocks, Todd thought as their tour group gathered around the guide. He'd failed totally in the excuses-not-to-go-on-the-tour department and now, here he was, sweating in the jungle instead of skin-diving in the cool water.

The tour guide, Eduardo, was a tiny, delicate-boned creature with huge, pale-colored eyes that made Todd immensely uneasy—they seemed to look right through him in a peculiarly disconcerting way.

Mimsey, however, was in her element, climbing around on the rocks like a kid. Todd watched her scramble up a small pile of ruins in her khaki pseudo-archaeologist's outfit, a wide grin on her sweaty face, and found himself wondering for all he was worth where he'd come from. Between her and his father—despite how opposite they were, there seemed no genetic information to have come up with someone such as himself. Because both of them were kind of nerdy. And Todd was sure of one thing. He was not nerdy.

Right then his mother let out a howl.

Todd couldn't believe his eyes as her feet made flying treadmill motions, her arms flailing. She toppled from the rocks and fell ten feet straight into the guide's arms.

"*Ohh!*" everyone said.

How had that little guy gotten over there so fast? How had he caught his mother? How had his tiny body withstood the impact?

Eduardo calmly placed Mimsey, sitting, on the ground.

"Th-thank you," she said, wobbly-voiced.

Everyone hurried over and asked her if she was all right. Everyone but Todd, who was too shocked to move, and Brad, who had already found a tree to sit under and had pulled his pocket organizer out and was completely engrossed.

"That *creature*, that *thing!*" Mimsey looked up at the crowd around her. "I didn't know it was there and I almost stepped on it!"

"What thing?" a woman asked.

"The iguana," Eduardo answered. "It's good that you did not step on it ...."

"Very good," Mimsey looked down at her spanking new hiking boots.

".... there's a legend about the iguanas at Cozumel," Eduardo continued. "The iguana is a patient creature. Some people call it lazy, but they show they don't know about spiritual things. It is said that these iguanas are the spirits of the ancient Mayan women who have returned to their sacred shrine. They called this island Ah-Cuzamil-Peten, the Island of Swallows.

"The women would journey from the mainland by boat to worship Ix-Chel, the goddess of fertility. They made figurines of the child they hoped to have and give the figurines as offerings to the great goddess. Archaeological digs still unearth these little figurines from time to time."

Eduardo's voice poured like warm honey over the hot air. His huge eyes, never blinking, took in everyone, without looking at anyone. Except, Todd noticed, first his mother, and then himself.

"The iguanas permit us to visit their holy place, but you must be very careful to treat them with respect, as the consequences are severe."

"They aren't poisonous, are they?" One of the women asked, her voice quavering.

"No." Eduardo offered Mimsey his hand and she stood unsteadily. "They don't resort to such obvious tactics. They have greater powers."

"Such as what?" Mimsey asked.

"Some say that those who do not respect the iguana are turned to stone here at the ruins. Others say that they turn disrespectful people into iguanas, so they can know themselves what it is not to be respected when someone harasses them."

Todd found this legend stuff pretty darn boring, and besides that, just as he'd predicted, the day was hot and humid. He joined his father under the tree. Dad seemed to be perfectly happy, involved in his pocket organizer. Todd wished he had one, he could see right off that it had a lot of potential for cross-referencing girls.

The tour group ambled out of sight and it was a few minutes before Todd realized that Mom had followed after Eduardo without even giving a backwards glance toward him. Was it possible? It was too good to be true.

The minutes oozed past in a thick stillness. Todd felt a languid change in the air around him, it seemed to thicken and slow, the sun radiated a brittle, severe light that made the edges of everything appear to break apart and float off, melting, into the vermilion light. A hot stillness hung everywhere as though the whole ruin site were an unfriendly diorama. Dad had fallen asleep, pocket organizer in hand.

Then Todd saw movement out of the corner of his eye. He was amazed to see a company of iguanas sunning themselves on a pile of rocks six or seven feet away. There were maybe twenty of them. Todd couldn't believe his eyes—the huge reptiles appeared to materialize from nowhere.

Why, Todd wondered, were they all watching him? It was hugely disconcerting and he didn't like it one little bit. He made a sudden waving motion, hoping to scare them off, but they didn't even blink.

"Maybe they can't blink," Todd thought. He stood and walked stealthily toward them. They didn't budge, except to cock their heads and flick their fat, pink tongues.

What surprised Todd about their appearance, aside from how huge they were, was that their pupils were black and round, like human pupils, instead of vertical slits like he expected. Their flicking tongues looked sort of human too, pink and rounded, not forked. Some of them even looked like they were smiling.

"It's just the way their mouths are made," Todd argued with himself. But no, not all of them looked like they were smiling. That one in particular—it was *really* smirking at him. It didn't take its eyes off him, it followed his every move, and it was absolutely smirking.

Todd felt his anger rising, a hot anger, a vermilion anger, pouring through him like the hot sunlight. It poured all through him, and the more he looked at that iguana smirk, the more he felt his anger rising over the obsessive smotheration of his mother, the oblivion of his father, the illusiveness of beautiful girls, the frustration of childhood, the fear of adulthood, and the plain, oppressive, cloying, unbreathable heat of the moment.

He reached the smirking iguana. Of the crowd of lolling, sprawling iguanas, it was the smallest, only about two feet long. Todd stooped over and picked it up. It offered no resistance and Todd struggled in his mind what he was going to do with it.

At that moment, he heard Eduardo's voice. The tour group was returning, and with them, the ordinary day seemed to sieve back into Todd's consciousness as if squeezed through cheesecloth.

Feeling strange and disoriented, he became consciously aware of holding an iguana, the creature passive in his arms. Todd could hardly imagine what had given him the courage to approach it, let alone pick it up and hold it like a puppy.

It cocked its head at him. Todd saw into its intelligent, perceptive eyes, and wondered at what the iguana knew.

It was beautiful, with a terrible beauty—a brownish-green, with a neat row of spines down its back, its square head and neck decorated with dewlap and a fabulous pattern of various shades of the brown-green among it scales.

Eduardo's voice came closer, then Todd heard Mimsey's voice, and he knew what he would do. He carried the iguana back over to the tree where his father continued to sleep, finger poised over his pocket organizer.

Todd sat on the ground and hid the iguana behind the tree, holding onto it by its neck, although it made no struggle to get away. The tour group returned, and Mimsey, face flushed and radiating with sweat and smiles, came over to Todd, while the rest of the group gathered around Eduardo.

"You missed out on the most interesting stories!" she said, full of delight. "The Mayans were...."

Todd pulled the iguana out from behind the tree and thrust it at Mimsey. He was chuckling inside. This ought to really give her a scare! He waited for her to scream. But it wasn't her scream he heard—it was, somehow, his own.

He was on all fours, in the dirt, the wind knocked out of him. He tried to breathe the hot air and for a few seconds, he couldn't breathe at all. Then suddenly the breaths came, odd and slow. He could see every grain of dirt, in fabulous colors. How could dirt be so beautiful? Slowly he moved to pick himself up, but his arms were at all odds and angles, stretched out above his head. His legs too, were as if they were broken, jutting out sideways from his pelvis, but he was in no pain. It must, somehow, be the heat that made him feel so strange.

And then, Mom surely started to scream. She screamed and screamed, and Todd could not comprehend the frightening weirdness of the sound. All he knew was, he wanted to get away from it. It crawled into his head and beat around in chambers he'd never felt before. And even the way he found himself thinking was absolutely peculiar, slow, yet deep. Even as the sound of his mother's screaming felt like it would make something in his head explode, at the same time it was an ancient, but very familiar sound, that he'd not heard in hundreds of years.

Suddenly the view of everything changed and Todd realized he'd been picked up. He was turned around and found himself staring eye-to-eye into Eduardo's huge green eyes.

Todd saw Dad standing next to Mom. Dad's expression was bemused and confused and Mom ... something in Todd had a wisdom that was not Todd's own, it told him that Mom was in shock. She was looking *right at him* as if she had no idea who he was.

Eduardo turned to the tour group. "Everything is all right," he said in his honey-voice. "You'll all take the bus back to town." Then Eduardo talked rapidly to the bus driver. Todd knew this language even better than the other language—sweet, warm Mayan. It gave him an immense comfort, like warm sand on a cold night.

"Take them back," Eduardo said to the driver. "Then return with a car to get us."

The driver nodded, and left with the group.

Eduardo carried Todd to a shady spot and his parents followed. They all sat. "Did I not say, do not harm or hurt or tease or disrespect the iguana?"

Mimsey nodded emphatically. "You did! You did!"

"You see the result?"

Mimsey nodded wildly.

"I don't understand," Brad said. "Where's Todd?"

"This is Todd," Mom said, waving at him.

Todd was relieved that she'd stopped looking at him as though she'd never seen him. "This ... this iguana."

Iguana?!

Finally Todd looked down at his arms which were not arms and turned his head around—he caught sight of the spines running down his back, he felt the dewlap at his throat and it seemed that he was flicking his tongue in and out of his mouth. Horrors!

"Have you lost your mind?" Brad asked Mimsey.

"She has not lost her mind," Eduardo assured Brad.

"But what can we do?" Mimsey asked. "How can we get Todd back?"

"It cannot be done, little mother," Eduardo consoled. "What you must decide now is if you want to leave him here or take him home with you. I can arrange everything if you want to take him back. I'll teach you everything about his needs, how to provide the best environment for him."

"Leave him here? I couldn't even consider it. My goodness, he's my son!"

Todd saw the edge of horror in Mom's eyes soften and change into the devoted, needy look she always had for him.

"This is beyond ridiculous, Mimsey," Brad said.

"Brad—look—look into his eyes."

Mimsey picked Todd up and held him close to Dad. He pulled back, but then met Todd's stare.

"*Oh... my... god!*" Dad whispered.

*   *

It was a couple of days before everything was organized, but then, finally, they were at the airport, Eduardo wishing them well. Mimsey made quite a production out of the fact that *now* she had six carry-on pieces of luggage, and it felt just right.

At home Todd had the free run of the house, and Brad and Mimsey set up heat lamps in his favorite corners. He found that he didn't think too much about girls anymore, and he really wasn't too disappointed not to be going away to college. He found he had a lot of other, deeper and older things to think about.

His biggest problem was the same as ever. Mom still smothered him, and now he'd probably never get away from that. But, philosophically, he told himself, there were worse things than being constantly told that one was the most beautiful iguana on earth.

END

Stone Face

A short story by award winning author

Blythe Ayne

Stone Face

Alesia found herself again standing at her long, old, bubbly-glassed office window, mesmerized by the black storm pouring out its torrents and wind and sheer lonely darkness from a sky that roiled above the narrow canyon of office buildings. Lightning tore madly at the sky, followed by shockwaves of thunder which she felt beneath her flesh and deep in her bones.

But even while frightened by the drama of the living elements, Alesia's attention was taken by a row of gargoyles on the building across the street, at the edge between the dimension of office buildings and a long day of boring routine, and that other elemental reality—animate wind, electricity, crashing clouds, pelting water ... a powerful, angry dimension, oblivious of the creatures in the buildings below.

The gargoyles sat, squatted, hunched, and leered at the elements that beat upon them, and they leered at the creatures in their climate-safe cubicles. The hound dogs of hell, Alesia thought, scoffing at anything, everyone, including themselves, as water gushed from their mouths and poured into an intricate system of downspouts.

That's to say, all except one. Alesia's attention was entirely captivated by the one at the corner of the building, a worried, humanoid creature, a blue cast to it's cracked stone body, a furrowed brow with deep, deep set eyes—so deep, as if what it knew would be too much for any other creature to see without the protective protrusion of its bony brow.

Its high cheekbones, long, protruding, pointed ears and a thin-lipped grimace pulled at Alesia's overly kind heart, its limbs contorted around it's torso, holding up the corner of the building. Never a moment's rest! she thought. No water gushed from its mouth, and Alesia had an image of it fairly bursting from containment of the deluge.

The thought haunted her as she returned her attention to her work. Even its deep bony stare seemed to fix on her. Finally she put on her dark gray trench coat, deciding to take an early lunch. She took the elevator down to the street, joining the few people who scurried about in the downpour. She crossed the street, took the elevator to the top floor, walked down the empty hall to the end where a sign read, "To Roof—No Admittance."

She tried the door, expecting it to be locked. But, surprisingly, it was not. She climbed a short flight of stairs to another door, pushed it open against the force of the wind and stepped out on the gravelly roof.

The wind sucked her breath away while her coat whipped around her like a ship's sail, threatening to fling her into the tempestuous sky. She struggled to the edge of the building and, peering through the pointed stone spires, spied the row of gargoyles. The gutter that fed her stony friend was jammed with debris—twigs, leaves, and a burbling mud. As she leaned over the edge of the building, casting her glance at the street far below, and reeled from the vertigo—what was she doing here? She was more frightened of heights than anyone she knew.

But as she regained her balance and turned to leave, her attention was again riveted to the little gargoyle—it seemed to have moved an elbow. It's the flashing of the lightning making shadows leap about, she reasoned.

But even so, she found herself reaching through the stone spires, grabbing at the twigs and leaves and muck, throwing them from the gutter, reaching farther and farther from the back of the creature's throat towards his mouth, grabbing and thrusting, unable to see what she was accomplishing, just digging and flinging, digging and flinging, until, suddenly, a great inhalation of wind threw her backwards onto the roof.

She landed, sprawling, gasping for air, soaking wet, fingernails broken, blood from her fingers mixing with the downpour and running onto the gravelly floor of the roof. She held her hand in front of her face watching the blood flow.

There was a thud beside her. She was looking, through the sheet of rain, into the deep, deep eyes of the animated gargoyle.

"*YOU GAVE ME LIFE!*" He danced stiffly around her. "You not only gave me back my stone life ... I can't tell you how long my wind pipe has been stuck, years and years, decades, even. But you gave me *BLOOD!* You gave me breathing *LIFE!* Ohh, those looks we've exchanged, I knew you cared, but I didn't know you'd give me blood ... give me *LIFE!*"

"Ahm, well ... Mr. Gargoyle, I, uh, I didn't really *mean* to, ah, give you life." Alesia attempted to pull herself together, or at least sit more lady-like, if there was such a thing on a roof in a gale storm. She looked into the eyes of the grinning, dancing gnome, and watched as the old sadness came back into them. She felt her heart crumble into weakness. "That is, I was, I mean, I did *feel* something for you, but I certainly had no idea you'd ... you'd actually come to life!"

He sat cross-legged in front of her, looking serious. "You don't want me?"

"Want you? What would I do with you?"

"Why, anything you please. I'm yours to do with as you please."

"Really?"

"Absolutely. You gave me life. My life is yours."

"What if it pleases me to see you on the corner of this building every day, just as you were, except now, you know, able to do you job."

A sadness centuries old fell on his features. "I would do as you please."

*   *

Alesia was late returning to work after lunch. After she'd come down from the roof she'd gone shopping for pillows, of all things, and then she'd had to spend some little while in the ladies room attempting damage control to her hair, make-up, and a bit of slap-dash polish on her nails. She stuffed the two huge pillows into one of the gigantic bags they'd come in, then lugged her possessions back to her cubicle.

"What a day to go shopping!" Marsha, in the next cubicle, commented, fingers flying over her keyboard. "What'd you get?" She glanced at Alesia's two huge bags.

"Oh, just some pillows and an *objet d'art*."

"Let me see." Before Alesia could stop her, Marsha had rolled her chair over and was peeking in the bag. "A gargoyle? Well, not my sort of thing ...." she shrugged. "Incredible eyes, though! It'd be great in a flower garden. Must have cost a fortune!"

"Oh, just a little blood ... without the sweat and tears."

Marsha looked at her, bemused, giggled faintly and returned to her typing, while Alesia neatly folded down the top of the shopping bag.

END

My Gift for You ....

Go to URL: *bit.ly/RV_Park* to download the short story, *RV Park*, and to receive my newsletter *Home of the Heart*, which comes out occasionally—with giveaways, updates on my stories and books, and other miscellaneous goodies!

About the Author ....

I live in a forest with a few domestic and numerous wild creatures, where I create an ever-growing inventory of books, both nonfiction and fiction, short stories, illustrated kid's books, and articles, with a bit of wood carving when I need a change of pace.

I received my Doctorate from the University of California at Irvine in the School of Social Sciences, majoring in psychology and ethnography, after which I moved to the Pacific Northwest to write and to have a modest private psychotherapy practice in a small town not much bigger than a village. Finally I decided it was time to put my full focus on my writing, where, through the world-shrinking internet, I could "meet" greater numbers of people. *Where I could meet you!*

I Wish You Happiness, Health, Peace, and Joy,
Blythe

Questions, comments? I'd love to hear from you!:

Blythe@BlytheAyne.com

www.BlytheAyne.com